SEDUCED BY A CAJUN WEREWOLF

A STORMY WEATHER STORY

SELENA BLAKE

ECILA MEDIA CORP

A Stormy Weather Story - Book 3
Seduced by a Cajun Werewolf - Laurent & Violet

All rights reserved.

Copyright ©2008 Selena Blake

This book is a work of fiction. Any resemblance to persons, living or dead, places or events is purely coincidental. Characters, events, and organizations within this work are products of the author's imagination and are used fictitiously.

Let's Hook Up ;)

selena@selena-blake.com
http://www.selena-blake.com

Selena's FB Fan Group
https://www.facebook.com/groups/SelenaBlakeFanClub/

Selena on Twitter
http://www.twitter.com/selenablake

Selena on Instagram
https://www.instagram.com/selenaablake/

Don't Miss a Thing

Join Selena's mailing list and get news, sales, giveaways and a copy of her paranormal romance novel, Ready & Willing.

ABOUT SEDUCED BY A CAJUN WEREWOLF

On the outside, wealthy werewolf Laurent Deveraux has it all. A close-knit family. Immortality. Good looks. More money than he could ever spend. But none of that matters when the love of his life died so long ago.

Life is all about going through the motions until he comes face to face with the woman who haunts his dreams.

Cayenne doesn't know why she dreams of the wickedly handsome werewolf, but she intends to find out. Before she can get her answers, her past catches up with her in an explosive fashion. Now they're both on the run.

To survive and unbind her memories, they'll have to learn to trust each other again. Easier said than done.

But Laurent will do whatever it takes because he lost her once. He won't lose her again.

DEDICATION

To my Word War buddies. You know who you are. Thanks for all the pushing, cracking of the whip, and support. You guys rock.

PROLOGUE

FRANCE, 200 years ago

As beauties went, Violet de Barbarac was the loveliest of them all, inside and out. Laurent Deveraux watched, spellbound, as she cuddled a barn kitten to her chest. Jealousy filled him as she nuzzled the little feline's fur.

Oh, how he longed to feel her affections himself.

She looked up and as their gazes locked the world and all the problems in it melted away. As if seeing him had made her day, she offered him a smile that made his breath catch.

Laurent's heart beat faster as she approached. The brown ringlets of her hair shone in the late afternoon light. The lilac muslin of her dress molded her curves, complimenting her fair skin and her brilliant blue eyes.

He was fairly certain that she could have worn

a sack and looked just as beautiful. In fact, he lost all notice of anything but her eyes and the smile that lit his soul on fire.

"*Bonjour.*" Her voice was soft, pure. A solace in a crazy world.

"*Bonjour, belle dame,*" he greeted her. Her smile grew wider. He dreamed of that smile. Of those lips. Thoughts of her kept him awake at night. She was also the one thing that haunted his dreams when he did manage to fall asleep.

Unable to help himself, he reached for her hand, kissing the back. She'd removed her gloves and her skin was so soft, so warm against his, scented by rose petals. He turned her hand over and kissed the palm. Such perfect hands. Small, elegant, yet strong.

She seemed to glow with happiness.

The beast inside him demanded he carry her off and make her his. But the man knew he must win her. Woo her. Court her properly.

But propriety was the last thing on his mind when she reached up and caressed his cheek.

How could she touch him like that, knowing what he was? Humbled, he closed his eyes and soaked in the moment. She wasn't afraid of him. She'd told him as much. He found her bravery in the face of danger amazing.

He was the most blessed man in all of France.

"I can't stay long," she murmured regretfully.

"I know." They never seemed to have enough

time together. Each moment he spent in her company was bittersweet.

One day soon he would leave the Pack and make her his wife. And then he'd never have to be parted from her. Not for a single moment. She would make him laugh for hours at a time, they would talk as long as they wished, and at last, he wouldn't have to keep his hands to himself.

Lovesick, his brother called it. Laurent was happy to be lovesick. It was the most wondrous of feelings. One he prayed he never lost.

"Someone to keep you company." She held the kitten to his chest. The tiny creature let out a delicate mew.

"*Quoi?*" He frowned. He didn't need the company of a kitten. He needed her.

He cupped the kitten in his palm and looked down into tiny, trusting green eyes.

"Just until we can be together."

Until we can be together. Such wonderful words.

"Violet…"

She held a finger against his lips. It took everything he had not to scoop her up into his arms. Forget the kitten, he wanted to hold her. He wanted to feel her skin against his. A purring feline could never take her place, no matter how sweetly it snuggled against his chest.

She started to say something but her mother called from a distance.

Violet's cheeks turned a delightful rosy shade. What was she thinking?

"*Cheri...*" He sighed, not wanting to let her go.

She lingered for several long moments, obviously not wanting to leave him. Then she raised up on her toes. He dipped his head as his heart hammered in his chest.

He'd been waiting for this kiss forever it seemed. But he didn't want to rush her, scare her away. He slid his free hand around her waist.

"Laurent..." She sounded breathless. That made two of them.

"*Oui?*"

"*Je—je t'aime.*"

And there they were. The words he lived to hear. Sweet words of love. "Oh, *mon amour.*"

He leaned in to steal that kiss when her mother called again.

"I must go," she whispered quickly and stepped back. The only thing that kept his world from crumbling was the tiny smile curling her lips upward.

"Until we're together again, *cheri.*" He kissed her hand again, bereft to let her go.

She stepped away slowly, until their fingers barely touched. Her gaze dropped to the little orange kitten against his chest. Then she offered him one last smile before turning toward home.

Laurent knew he'd dream of that smile

tonight. Her touch, her words would feed him until he could see her again.

He stood there, rooted to the ground until he could no longer see her lovely form striding across the earth. The kitten let out a soft mew and snuggled closer.

He stroked the kitten's soft fur and held it out to look it over. Orange all over with a white belly and paws.

"*Il est juste toi et moi mon petit,*" he murmured. Just you. And me. Until they could make Violet a permanent part of the family.

The kitten purred.

A NOISE WOKE Laurent from a blissful dream.

"*Vite vite.* Come quick!" his brother called.

The urgency in his voice brought Laurent awake. He tugged on his trousers, shoved his feet into his shoes and grabbed a shirt on his way out the door.

Burke was already in the yard. A warm glow lit the sky, bringing Laurent to a stop. *Non. Dieu, non.*

They raced up the ridge. Laurent's heart stopped when he saw Violet's home swallowed by flames. He staggered but for a moment. Burke placed a steadying hand on his shoulder as he gasped for breath, every fiber in his being ready to shrivel with panic. But he couldn't. He had to get to her.

Laurent ran down the hill as fast as his legs would carry him. His cousins were already there. Sebastian looked grim. He dispatched André and Jules to search for the De Barbaracs.

Laurent started after them but came to a halt when he saw a crumpled form only a handful of steps outside the front door. Smoke burned his eyes as he approached. Violet's father, throat slashed, blood soaking the soil.

"*Non!*" he roared and charged toward the house. Sebastian and Burke caught him by the shoulders, holding him back. "*Non.*" He struggled against their hold, his very life flashing before his eyes.

"Violet! Violet!" The beast inside him pushed forward, cracking his bones, stretching his muscles, giving him strength.

Sebastian wrapped an arm around him from behind, holding him stationary. Tears filled Laurent's eyes as he fought. He had to save her. He could save her.

"Let go," he ground out.

"You can't save her," Burke shouted over the roar of the fire.

Laurent felt sick to his stomach. He could smell burning flesh on the air.

"They're looking for her, cousin," Sebastian offered. "Surely she escaped."

Sebastian's quiet words soothed his beast for an instant. Yes. She was smart. Strong. She would have escaped.

But no sooner had his cousin spoken than André came around one side of the house. Jules, the other.

"Did you find them?" Sebastian called.

"*Non*," Jules called. André shook his head, his mouth set in a grim line.

"No! Let me go. I can find her," Laurent cried. He strained, reaching for the house as if he could reach inside and pluck them out.

But inside he was dying. Shriveling. He sank to his knees, sobs wracking his body, tears blinding him. "No! *Dieu. Non.*"

And then the heavens opened and rain poured over the earth. The Fates cried with him.

1

New Orleans, present day

The Smokestack bar on the corner of Iberville and Decatur overflowed with locals, tourists, and thick cigarette smoke but Laurent Deveraux still felt alone. Seated at a small round table in the back corner of the dark room, he nursed a glass of whiskey. A moody blues ballad reverberated off the walls and soaked into his bones.

"Slow down there, buddy," Burke said as Laurent drained his glass. "Leave some for the rest of us."

"I doubt New Orleans is suddenly going to run out of whiskey, brother," Laurent said wryly.

Burke cut him a look. "What crawled up yer butt and died?"

"Nothing," he muttered.

He envied his brother's easy going attitude. Burke sat with his long legs stretched out in front of him as if he didn't have a care in the world. He moved his feet to the music and smiled when the waitress stopped by their table for the fifth time that night.

Laurent took another sip of whiskey. Would he ever be happy like that again? Most of the year he managed to shake himself from his funk. But not today.

His inner wolf felt caged. He wasn't known for keeping his temper leashed. What he needed was a good fuck.

He surveyed the crowd, his gaze falling on the females. He worked his jaw back and forth as he looked them over and dismissed them all just as quickly.

None of them were *her*.

And this close to the anniversary of her disappearance, no one else would do.

With Sebastian and Jules mated, their pack was growing larger, and at the same time, shrinking. Each time he saw his cousins with their women, *Dieu*, they reminded him of what he'd never have.

It was damn near impossible to go a whole day without hearing the women's laughter or see the love shining in their eyes. Laurent didn't blame them, didn't begrudge them their happiness, but he couldn't help but think of everything he'd lost.

Laurent shoved the thought into the back of his mind and gulped down another sip of the amber liquid. Relishing the fire that scalded his throat, he prayed for forgetfulness. The band's lead singer strummed the guitar with old weathered hands and sang from his soul—of loss, hope, and loneliness.

All things Laurent was intimately familiar with.

A mellow jazz tune filled the room and the hot breeze blew into the space like a blow torch. A single figure cloaked in darkness entered and crossed Laurent's line of sight. The woman kept to the shadows and settled at a table in the opposite corner. She was dressed in black from head to toe, and Laurent immediately discarded her as Goth or a wanna-be vamp. Plenty of those lived in the city.

But then the scent of roses wafted under his nose, tickling his memory. He crossed his arms over his chest and pushed the recollection away. Only, it didn't want to go. It remained as fresh in his mind as it had the first time he'd smelled that sweet floral scent. Two hundred years did little to erase the memory of that day.

Or of *her*.

Long brunette curls framed her angelic face, and she had the brightest blue eyes he'd ever seen.

They changed with her mood. And her smile, *Dieu*, her smile could charm even the most chaste saint. Her image flashed before him like a blip on the television screen.

Laurent shook his head.

"You all right, cousin?" André asked in that quiet, deep voice.

Laurent nodded. "You guys should go on home. You don't have to stay with me."

"You sure?" Burke finished off his beer.

He nodded. "I'll get the bill." After all, he'd done the most drinking.

They stared at him for a moment, and then got to their feet. He watched them depart. Lifted a hand to wave goodbye. Then tossed back another shot of whiskey.

Damn his high metabolism.

Laurent savored the darker hours, when he felt most at peace, closest to his true self. These were the hours during which he didn't have to work so hard to hide.

Electricity sizzled through the bar, and cold fingers tried to reach into his mind. He slammed the door shut on his thoughts and looked around the room suspiciously, his gaze falling on the newcomer in black. A ray of light sliced across the room, briefly highlighting the woman's face. Brilliant blue eyes met his, and he sucked in a breath.

No. It wasn't possible. He struggled with the

reality of what he'd seen...and of what he knew to be true.

And just like that, the light was gone—and so was she.

What the hell?

He narrowed his gaze on the empty chair, and then glanced around the room. Was it possible she wasn't just a gothic chick? Was it possible...no, he wouldn't put a name to it. Wouldn't think that thought. It was better for his sanity if he told himself she was dead.

He finished his whiskey, tossed several bills onto the table, and headed for the door.

Even in the middle of the night, the streets of New Orleans were bathed in heat and humidity; both wrapped around him like a wet wool coat.

Sex, sweat, and exhaust swirled together in a combination that was distinctively French Quarter. Thunder rumbled overhead as he started down the uneven sidewalk and the hairs on the back of his neck tingled in warning.

He stuck to the shadows; his hands in his pockets, his pace decidedly laggard. Ever since he'd moved here from France, he'd been amazed by how alive the city was even after dark, with dangers lurking around every corner. Bars were open till dawn, and party goers danced all night.

Stepping across the street, he headed northwest through an alley. The wind picked up, and he lifted his face to the sky. It would rain soon; he could smell it and he welcomed it.

The city lights blocked out most of the stars, but he could just make out the moon as it danced through the clouds.

A raindrop hit his cheek. Then another. And slowly more and more droplets rained down. Big, fat, Texas-sized drops. Commotion filled the streets as people ran for cover. He forged on, not even bothering to quicken his steps.

As he crossed another cobble-lined street, a stealthy figure in his peripheral view caught his attention. He turned and took in the curvy form in the long black coat. The hood hid her face from the light, but two aqua eyes glowed at him from the inky darkness. Cool fingers tickled his mind again, and he decided to let her in just enough to find out what she wanted with him.

What do you want?

She said nothing. Not aloud, nor in his mind.

Instead, she stepped from the shadows and strode into the middle of the street, her boots coming together as she stopped with almost military precision. She seemed almost a silhouette. Not quite real, but not an illusion, either.

Laurent's breathing quickened, as did his heartbeat. His body tightened, going on full alert, and his inner wolf crept forward, slowly taking over his human senses.

He couldn't hear her heartbeat. Perhaps she

didn't have one. She clearly was in no rush to tell him why she was stalking him.

The rain fell in heavy drops, but she didn't seem to notice. In the dim light of the street lamps, he could see her clearly now. Slowly, she lifted her hands and pushed back the thick fabric hiding her face. She was almost too beautiful to look at—and yet, Laurent couldn't look away.

He knew that face as well as he knew his own.

His breath left his lungs in a rush. Her skin was still dewy and perfect, like that of a fine porcelain doll. *Ethereal.* Her brows were perfect arches, the same charcoal brown he'd been fascinated by all those years ago. Even in the darkness, he could make out the thick lashes that fringed her eyes.

Those eyes...so blue, so beautiful. He felt like he'd been kicked in the gut by a mule. Damn, she was beautiful.

What was she doing standing in the middle of a street in New Orleans when she'd died two hundred years ago in France?

His arms and legs felt heavy; he was getting drenched. But it didn't matter. He'd stand in a hurricane if it meant finding out if she, if *Violet*, were real. Or if he'd finally lost his mind and was only envisioning her.

Her lips were just as rosy as he remembered; her nose as perfectly shaped, her face oval and oh so familiar.

She remained silent. Did she recognize him?

He stepped closer, silently praying to the gods, Fates, and anyone else who would listen. Sniffing the air, he tried to catch her scent but she was downwind.

"Violet?" He didn't like the husky tone of his voice. Hated the weakness in his knees, the soreness that resided where his heart had once been. Loathed the desire he still felt for a woman long dead.

Could his eyes be playing tricks on him? Could this woman really be his little Violet? After all these years?

Not trusting himself or his luck, he took another step. She lifted her hands to her lips, almost as if she were praying. Her fingernails were long and polished a glossy red.

A sharp ache erupted inside his chest, and he reached up to rub it. His hand brushed something, and he looked down to see a dart sticking out of his skin. Plucking it out, he stared at the woman before him. Then she and the rest of the world went dark.

2

Laurent woke slowly. His arms and legs were numb, and his joints ached. He propped one eye open, then the other, and found himself staring at an unfamiliar ceiling made of concrete, with a fan high overhead. Pain spiked in his temples, and he ground his teeth together. What the hell had happened to him?

Disoriented, he tried to remember where he was and how he'd gotten here. He lifted his head and surveyed his surroundings. He was in a large bedroom, by the looks of it.

The furnishings were elegant and sleek, if somewhat sparse for the large space. Across from the bed, a pair of French doors stood open, revealing a balcony.

Rain pattered outside. He smelled its freshness and the accompanying humidity filled his lungs.

What he wouldn't give for a sip of rainwater right now.

Street lamps illuminated the rain splattered concrete. No lights were on inside his cement prison, but that didn't bother him as much as the fact that cold steel bit into his wrists. He craned his neck to get a better look.

Fuck. This was not good.

How had it happened? He searched his memory and remembered the shadowy form and the dart in his chest. Then, blackness. How in hell had he let himself be captured?

The simple answer was…*her.* He'd been so surprised to see her that he'd let down his guard. Where was she? How was it that she was still alive?

Damn, his head hurt. Had he just imagined her? Had he let himself believe it was her when it wasn't? Had he put her face on another woman's body? Perhaps he'd been kidnapped for a ransom. It wasn't as if Sebastian had been low key about their wealth these past few years.

Or maybe he'd been taken by a competing company. Not that it mattered right now. He had to get out of here.

His wolf rushed forward, and he braced himself for the change that would snap his bones and stretch his muscles. He gave in to the power that would free him.

His captor stepped into the open doorway, the lights from the street silhouetting her lithe form.

"Sorry about the heat," she said but didn't sound remorseful. "Storm caused a power surge that knocked out the air conditioner."

He pulled back the reins on his wolf. "Let me go, Violet."

She made a *tsking* sound and cocked her head to one side. When she made no move to free him, he pulled at the chains. They rattled and clanked but didn't budge.

"That's not my name," she said in French, her tone soft, lyrical. Though she denied it, she couldn't fake her voice. Couldn't change or hide it. And he'd never forgotten it. Never forgotten her laugh or anything else about her. Not her goodness. Not her kindness. Not the gentle way she'd plucked a splinter from his palm one afternoon in mid Spring.

Although she sounded the same, her words carried an icy edge, reminding him that she was not the delicate flower he remembered.

"Well, whatever your name is, let me go." If she didn't have such an odd look in her eye, he might question his determination to get *out* of her bed.

"That's not going to happen."

She sounded so calm. Eerily calm. As if having a man tied to her bed was an everyday occurrence.

The thought brought on a wave of jealousy that threatened to overtake his rising ire. For two hundred years, he'd dreamed of having a second chance with this woman. He'd yearned for it, had wanted nothing else...and now he was tied to her bed.

"Why not?" he asked, testing the chains again. He knew he could probably just rip them apart, but a part of him wanted to know why she'd chained him...before he got loose.

But she denied who she was. Didn't seem to recognize him. Her resistance was just one more dagger to his chest. Damn the Fates and their bitter sense of humor.

"You have information I need."

He frowned. What kind of information could he possibly have?

She crossed her arms. "Your name, for starters."

"You know my name, sweetheart." A gust of wind brought a spattering of water droplets on his feet and lifted her hair into a dark cloud before letting it settle around her shoulders. The ebony strands were straight now, not curly. But he still remembered the silky softness of it against his fingertips. Remembered the brush of it against his lips.

"I'm *not* your sweetheart," she bit out.

At one time, she had been. "How is it that you're in New Orleans?"

"I was hired to do a job," she said simply. A

job? As a fashion designer, maybe. He took in her form fitting coat. It looked tailored to fit her, showing off the perfect indentation of her waist, the flair of her hips.

"I mean, this year. How is it possible that you're still alive? Your entire family was massacred two hundred years ago."

"I don't know what you're talking about, *monsieur*."

"Of course you don't," he said sarcastically. Why was she denying her past?

Before he could blink, she launched herself into the air and came down on top of him. She landed easily, with her knees on either side of his hips.

"Why do I dream of you?" she demanded in English. Her fingernails bit into his naked chest, and he hissed out a breath.

"I don't know. Why *do* you dream of me?" She dreamed of him? Yet she didn't know who he was? Nevertheless, the thought pleased him, and he was suddenly a little cocky.

She cut those aqua eyes at him and dug her nails a little deeper. "I don't have memories. But you and I have obviously met. Where? When?"

He stared up at her for a long time. A thousand times he'd dreamt of this. Of her, above him. But in his dream, she was riding his cock all the way to pleasure, not slicing and dicing him with her fingernails.

Could she really not know? She couldn't remember? He swallowed the venomous words that sprang to mind. They'd only bring more harm than good. He had to keep his cool.

The look in her eyes was cold and distant, yet inquisitive. She really didn't remember him. The crazy little sprig of hope that had blossomed inside his heart when he'd first seen her in the bar died a quick death. And as it did, his wolf snapped forward, lashing out at the pain.

It wasn't right; wasn't natural for a wolf to go his whole life without a mate. He'd decided long ago that if he couldn't have Violet, then he wouldn't take anyone as his other half. He couldn't. He *hadn't*.

And yet, here she was!

"We met in France two hundred years ago," he said. Bitterness dried his mouth, and he looked away. She was no longer the woman he'd once loved.

His patience wearing thin, he pulled hard at the chains.

"It won't help," she said. "They're reinforced."

"Too fucking bad. I'm not your hostage."

"Oh, but you are." She hiked her fingers up his chest, and he couldn't stop the shudder that wracked his body. As much as he hated being tied down, chained and immobile, he still loved her touch. He couldn't let her know that, though.

Wouldn't give her any more ammunition to use against him.

"What the fuck do you want?" He tried to ignore the way the apex of her thighs cradled his crotch. Failed to ignore the pale sliver of skin peaking from beneath the V of her coat.

"Your name."

"Why do you want to know?"

"I need to be sure I have the right man."

At one time, he'd been the right man. And she'd been the right woman. His heart ached because that time was gone. Stolen. Grains of sand, fallen through the hour glass. Or had they? Did the Fates, with their twisted sense of humor, believe in second chances?

"Are you supposed to give me a show? A little strip tease?" he taunted.

The smile she gave him made every muscle in his body tighten, from his throat to his toes. It was sexy, sultry, and even a little sadistic. She leaned closer and stared into his eyes.

She was all vixen. This side of her was completely different from the sweet, innocent girl he'd known. She still had the same angelic features, but her attitude was edgy and alluring.

"Would you like that?" She watched him closely.

He groaned low in his throat. She was just toying with him, but he couldn't stop his body's traitorous reaction. Could no longer ignore the way her thighs hugged him and held his cock prisoner against her. She rolled her hips, rubbing herself against him. His eyes rolled back.

"I just bet you would," she murmured. She sat back and regarded him for a moment. Then her hands went to the buttons of her coat.

He sucked in a breath and held it, his eyes following every movement of her elegant fingers. She popped one button open to reveal more skin. The next displayed the curve of her breasts. He licked his lips, wishing for more light so he wouldn't miss a single detail. Somewhere in the back of his mind, a siren blared. He ignored the warning that this could be a trick. Some witch or wizard playing with his mind. It didn't matter. This was the closest he'd ever come to being with her, and he couldn't stop now.

The final button popped free, and her coat hung open. His gaze traveled over the naked skin of her flat, lean stomach. Black lace clung to her breasts like a second skin. Dying to cup those perfect globes in his hands, he jerked at the chains.

Obviously startled, she sailed through the air, landing gently beside the bed. Her aerodynamics lead him to a single conclusion.

She was a vampiress.

3

North of New Orleans

Burke sipped his iced tea, relishing the cool liquid. The heat was oppressive this time of year, even at two am.

His brother had yet to return home and he was keeping vigil from the top porch, surveying the vast property of the Deveraux estate. The creatures of the night harmonized in a sweet song. Only in Louisiana…

"Why are you still up?"

André.

"Couldn't sleep. You?"

"Keep thinkin' about Laurent. He seemed so distant tonight."

Burke nodded at the empty chair beside him. André collapsed into it with a sigh.

"It's her," Burke said, knowing André wouldn't need an explanation.

"I know 'get over her' would be pointless advice," André said.

"Especially in this family," Burke agreed. Deveraux men loved their women forever. Together or not. Mated or not. And Laurent was suffering for it. Had been suffering for centuries.

"You don't think he got himself into trouble, do ya?"

Burke grunted and took another sip of his tea. "I wouldn't put it past him. He seems to go lookin' for trouble this time of year."

"Remember that time we had to pull him outta that bar in Baton Rouge?" André asked with a dry laugh.

They sat for a moment, the night silent save for the wildlife.

"I remember."

"I imagine it's gotta be harder for him," André said, putting the rocking chair into motion.

"Why's that?"

"Not knowing what happened to her."

"Yeah." Burke understood loss all too well. But in his case…at least he knew—He stopped his train of thought. "I think about that every so often. Wondering if he'd be different, feel different if he knew for sure what happened to her."

"I always hoped, for his sake, that she'd come

back one day. That she just ran for her life and it took her a while to find her way back to him."

"Or maybe it was post traumatic stress," Burke added, knowing how that felt too.

"Or maybe amnesia. It's possible she got conked on da head."

Burke let out a sigh. He'd thought of that too. He'd thought of a dozen different scenarios. Each one was plausible. But the more time passed, the more he thought Violet had been mortally wounded that night and they'd just never found her body. And that was the worst scenario of all.

It meant that Laurent would never know any peace.

Cayenne stared at the big man on her bed. His eyes were fixed on her body, and he watched her slide the coat from her shoulders like he would remember this moment forever. She smelled the desire coursing through his veins and wanted to taste it. She prided herself on feeling nothing at all, save for her usual hunger, so it was strange to feel a tendril of need deep in her own belly.

He was so familiar. And not just because he'd appeared in her dreams over the years. A hint of memory skittered through her mind. That pitch black, unruly hair. Those piercing black/brown eyes. Eyes meant to seduce and enchant. Eyes that now raked over her body like tiny hands, touching and caressing every inch he could see. Another tremor erupted in her belly, and she suddenly felt hot all over. She welcomed the warmth. Craved it, in fact.

Who *was* he? Why couldn't she remember? She put her hands on her hips and glared down at him. He was more than a mark. More than a bull's-eye at the end of her scope. He'd become more the moment he'd called her *Violet*. The name caused more memories to flutter...incomplete snippets that still alluded her. She'd track them down soon enough. Tracking was part of the game.

She shouldn't like how he was looking at her. As if she were a prized possession and he wanted her all to himself. She'd never slept with a target, and she wasn't going to start now. But damn, she was tempted.

"Now—you were telling me your name," she said, leaning against one of the tall square posts at the end of the bed. She let her eyes take a survey of their own, starting at his bare feet and moving up his hard, muscled legs. Well-worn denim, still damp from the rain, encased thighs she ached to touch. Then across his wide, hair-dusted chest. Every muscle was perfectly sculpted.

Tension and frustration radiated off of him as he pulled at the chains binding his wrists. The bed groaned under the stress, and she stifled a moan at the sight of his big biceps in full flex.

Cayenne gave herself a mental shake and straightened. She was here for a job, not a romp between the sheets. If she wanted that, all she had to do was head back to the French Quarter and find an unsuspecting tourist. Though there were plenty of mortals who would gladly offer themselves for her feeding, she wasn't hungry for them. She was hungry for *him*.

Him in all his fine glory, splayed out across the huge bed like a writhing fish on a platter. Lightning lit the room, lighting up his dark eyes. She held them with her own.

"Tell me *your* name first," he said, apparently giving up on the whole *Violet* thing.

Seeing no reason for him not to know her name, especially since he'd be dead in an hour or so anyway, she gripped the other bedpost and swung gently to the side. "My name is Cayenne Laroque."

"I'd say it's nice to meet you, Cayenne, but you shot me with a dart and chained me to your bed." He sounded angry, and rightfully so. She hadn't expected him to fall so easily.

Not that she'd expected to drug him and chain him to the bed, either. Doing so had been a last second decision on her part. This job was supposed to be quick and easy. Just like every single job she'd done for the last hundred and fifty three years.

Except this one was different. *He* was different. She'd watched him enough over the last two weeks to pick up plenty of character traits that set him apart from her usual targets.

He wasn't the usual swine she was sent to dispatch. He didn't have a wife he cheated on. Didn't beat children or animals. Wasn't a serial killer, from what she could tell. He didn't always put the toilet seat down, but in her opinion, that was hardly a reason to off someone.

But it wasn't her call.

She must really look like this Violet woman for him to let down his guard. Obviously he didn't know why she was here. He didn't seem the least bit nervous. Was he hiding his emotions? Or was he really that clueless?

If he discovered why she was here, would he beg for his life? So many men had. Weak men, who'd cried like little girls and screamed like women. There was no honor in dying so pathetically. Their pleas and bribes hadn't worked. She hadn't spared anyone; she'd only carried out each job.

The proud set of his jaw told her he would not beg for his life. Something dark and troubling filled in his eyes. A sorrow so deep, even she had a hard time commiserating with him. Not that she'd allowed herself to do so in the past two centuries. At least not since—No. She couldn't afford the weakness.

Emil had constantly reminded her that she

was weak simply because she was female. Anger boiled deep inside at the unwelcome memory, and her fangs lengthened.

Latching on to that dark, dangerous emotion, she flipped her hair over her shoulder. She had to remember all the terrible people she'd snuffed out in the past. Murderers, rapists, thieves. Men who'd given society nothing but pain.

She needed to focus.

"You said we met in France." She refused to be seduced by his gorgeous body or the intense pain in his eyes.

"Yes." He gritted his teeth. Anger vibrated off of him.

She suspected she'd feel the same way, were she in his position. "How did we know each other?"

"What's with all the questions? Don't you remember your own childhood?" Disbelief, pain, and longing filled his voice. "Don't you remember *me?*"

So that's why he was angry. He still believed she was Violet, denying her past. Their past.

"I have no memories at all." And no mercy, she reminded herself.

He stared at her for endless seconds, the only sound in the room was of rain pouring against the concrete balcony.

"How sad for you," he finally said. "You were a delightful little girl, with such big, brown curls.

It's a shame you straightened them. Your eyes were so blue, even the sky was jealous."

"Such poetic words." Words that spoke to what was left of her soul.

He met her eyes. "True words. You made friends wherever you went, *cheri*. With men, women, and children, who all fell under your spell. You were quite the charmer."

She stepped across the room to the open doors. Drops of water splattered her boots, but she didn't care.

"You grew up."

"And?" Her voice was so soft she wasn't sure if he'd even heard her, but she knew that what was said about werewolves was true. They had heightened senses.

"You became the most beautiful woman in all of France," he answered. She gave him a sharp look over her shoulder. Why had she asked? Why did she care? This was her life now. Her path was set. The past no longer mattered, certainly not after two hundred years. But if she could figure out exactly how they knew each other, perhaps she could get rid of the dreams. Lustful dreams that distracted her, consumed her, and left her with unfulfilled desires.

"You turned heads everywhere you went, *ma belle*. *Dieu*. " He cut off his words as if embarrassed by them. "I used to get so jealous—"

"We were...an item?"

"Something like that." His forehead creased in a frown. He stared up at the ceiling and took a long breath. She watched his massive chest rise and fall and felt a strong urge to place her hand over his heart. To ease the pained look that marred his handsome face. Not physical pain, but emotional. Like their conversation might, in fact, kill him.

She turned back to the storm lighting up the sky. Failure is not an option, she reminded herself. "Do you have any idea why I'm here?" she finally asked.

"No," he said. "But I've wished for it at least once a day for the last seventy-four thousand days." His words were honest, passionate, and defeated.

"Enough!" She spun and glared at him. "Your words will not alter your fate."

"I don't expect them to. Why are you here, Cayenne? Obviously something happened all those years ago. Something of which you have no memory. Which means you also have no memory of me. So why have you come?"

Even tied to the bed, flat on his back in what should have been a vulnerable position, he was making sense, taking control. She took another deep breath and started forward. She may not remember him, but she remembered her dreams. She knew the feel of his skin against hers, the way the coarse hair on his chest tickled her breasts.

She remembered the heat of his breath against her cheek as he whispered endearments to her in French.

Every sensation was as real as if they'd actually been together. But they hadn't. And so, the realism made her curious. Would his muscles ripple beneath her fingertips?

Her curiosity disgusted her. She wasn't used to being sidetracked. She was cold. Ruthless. Calculating. She didn't dawdle. Never allowed herself to participate in small talk. Why would she? The sooner she was done, the sooner she could leave.

But there was something about him. And, damn it, she wanted to find out what that something was.

4

Cayenne looked at Laurent with glowing blue eyes. He swallowed but didn't look away. Her glossy hair cascaded around her shoulders as she stalked toward him. She reminded him of a panther walking along a branch in the jungle, stalking her dinner.

He'd gladly offer himself for her table. Almost did, when she licked her lips and crawled onto the bed. She straddled his legs and slowly crept up his body, her gaze never leaving his. He couldn't have looked away if he'd wanted to.

Something about her was different. Maybe only a subtle shift in attitude, but he could feel it. Could see it in the tiny smirk on her lips. Lightning lit the sky, turning the darkness bright and bathed her in pale blue light. The rain continued to pour down and, a few seconds later, thunder rolled over the city like a run-away steel drum.

She stopped when her hand touched his shoulder. She had such cold fingers for such a hot night; they seared his overheated skin like icicles. A yearning deep inside made him want to hold her close and warm her up. Desire ran hot and fast through his body, and he couldn't stop it or deny the evidence she surely felt. Couldn't hold back the need he'd experienced for so long.

"I'll admit you intrigue me." She cocked her head to one side, as if she wasn't sure what to make of him. When had that sweet little girl become this sassy, insanely sexy woman? It didn't matter, he decided. He liked her sass. Yet he wondered if it was an act.

"What did I call you? All those years ago?"

"You called me Laurent."

"So you *are* Laurent Deveraux?" She leaned down and licked his chest. He closed his eyes and tried to memorize every detail, every sensation that washed over him.

"Yes."

"Good."

"Is it?"

"I wouldn't want to kill the wrong person." Her sultry pout belied her words. Kill? As in kill...*him?* That siren went off again in his head.

"Why would you want to kill me?"

"It's not what *I* want, dearest. It's what I was hired to do. It's how things work."

"Then why haven't you killed me yet?"

Her face the portrait of concentration, she raked her fingernails across his chest, and he sucked in a sharp breath. She lifted her hands and inspected the nail on her index finger. The seconds ticked by. What the hell was she thinking? What game was she playing?

"That's a good question, Laurent. A very good question." This time, when she aimed her fingernail above his heart, the muscle he'd thought was long gone actually skipped a beat. Momentarily he thought of turning, fighting, and getting the hell out of there. But he couldn't make himself do any of those things. Instead, he laughed.

"You find something funny about being chained to my bed, wolf?"

"I find it ironic that I've spent the better part of two hundred years trying to drink away your memory and here you are, almost to the day of your disappearance—tormenting me once again. I can't help but wonder if I'm dreaming."

"I can assure you wolf, you're not dreaming."

A sharp sting ripped through him as the red tip of one of her nails carved into his flesh like a knife. Not too deep, but far enough to make it bleed. He growled up at her. Any normal person would have been scared shitless, but she just laughed.

Then she sliced another line.

"An upside down cross...for the fallen ones."

"Do you mark all of your victims?" he asked.

Her gaze flicked to his, and then back to his chest. "No. You're the lucky first."

"Kiss me."

"What?" For a second, maybe even less, she looked rattled. Unsure of herself. The cocky smile that graced her lips disappeared.

"I told you to kiss me."

"And you think I'm going to follow your orders?" Sass and superiority flooded back into her beautiful azure eyes. "Just like that?"

"You know you want to," he taunted. And he knew he might just die if she didn't. He wanted to feel those dusky pink lips on his. Against his skin. Gliding over his stomach, wrapped around his cock. He went in for the kill. "I can see it in your eyes."

"You lie."

"Do I?" he asked.

She was looking at his lips.

Mentally, he pictured himself cupping her cheeks. Imagined the softness of her skin. He knew she'd be cold to the touch and wondered how long it would take for him to warm her. He wanted to haul her close and lavish her with kisses and caresses, to touch her until she remembered. Until she would never forget him again.

Instead, he settled for rotating his hips, effectively rubbing the hard length of his cock against the apex of her thighs.

She licked her lips and leaned forward. It was all he could do to stay relaxed against the bed, to not seem so anxious. The wolf inside him demanded he snap the chains and make her his. His more human half recognized the need to engage her if he had any hope of resurrecting their relationship.

He needed to seduce her.

"Go ahead," he said. "I won't bite."

"But *I* will, *monsieur*," she whispered, her lips only millimeters from his.

He sucked in a deep breath and held her gaze. Two hundred years he'd waited for this. Did she have any clue? Did she know he was ready to pass out from the ecstasy? But he wouldn't. He *couldn't*. Like hell, he'd miss this kiss.

"I was hoping you would," he whispered back. Then he closed the tiny distance between them.

The first tentative touch of her lips quenched his thirst. He pressed his body to hers. Her lithe frame and feminine curves fit against him from chest to crotch; she rested her hands on his shoulders and kissed him slowly, her movements exploratory. The delicate brushes of her lips became firmer, hotter.

He let her take the lead, accepted her weight as she sank down on him and wrapped an arm behind his neck. She opened her lips ever so slightly and hovered there, barely moving, as if waiting. Deciding something. Then her tongue swept along his lips, tasting and tempting him. He groaned.

She swallowed the sound and kissed him harder. Hot, open mouthed, her body grinding against his as if she couldn't get enough. He slid his tongue inside her mouth, let it parry with hers. She sucked it in deep and nibbled it with her teeth.

Not touching her was torture. The muscles in his arms, shoulders and chest ached, not just from the confinement, but from the desire to wrap around her and never let her go. Part of him felt weak and helpless. Violet was in his arms...or rather, she should have been. He was kissing her as he'd always wanted to do. Yet he didn't want to snap the chains and scare her away. The other part of him, the darker part, however, demanded that he do exactly that.

When she pulled back, her hair cascaded around them like a sleek, dark curtain. "You're right. I did want to do that."

"So do it again," he urged.

"Sorry, *monsieur*. It was a one-time deal."

"I don't think so, sweetie," he said. He knew she was lying; he could smell her arousal. But he could also smell something...darker. More toxic. Not anger or fear. He was losing his control over her mind. He stared pointedly at her lips. "That was the best kiss I've had in a *helluva* long time. I want another."

She didn't even look at him as she slithered off his lap. Her footsteps were barely audible over the loud bang of thunder. The storm outside crescendoed as she reached into her coat. He saw the hilt of a sword, then the sheen of its silver blade.

His heart exploded. With a single hard yank, he pulled free of the chains and leapt across the room.

She whirled with a surprised cry.

He grabbed her wrist before she could raise the sword, but miscalculated her strength. She jerked away from him and swung the weapon. He jumped back.

"I thought you were joking about the whole killing me thing." He held his hands out in a placating gesture and offered her a dazzling smile.

"I never joke." Her fangs were a brilliant white against her berry colored lips; her eyes, an eerie silver, swirled with emotions. She continued to attack.

"What the hell—" He dodged another swing. "—is wrong with you?"

Perhaps she was possessed. She moved around him like a firefly, wielding her weapon. He ducked. The blade came down on the dresser next to him, and the once contemporary piece splintered into bits of wood.

"You're strong, I'll give you that." He hurled himself across the bed.

She vaulted onto it, her sword held high, and

he attacked her. His tackle brought them down in a heap. The sword hit the ground with a clatter, and air whooshed out of her lungs.

"Wolf!" she snarled.

"Did you think I wouldn't go down fighting?" he asked. She strained against him, but he held her down. Years of service in several armies had taught him how to stay alive.

"You're supposed to die," she snapped. "It's ordered."

"Too fucking bad, princess." He rubbed his cheek against hers, relishing the softness of her skin, the subtle scent of woman and lotion.

"I've always wondered what happened to you. We never found your body." She lay coiled beneath him as tightly as a snake, ready to strike. But it was his turn to enjoy her. He licked her earlobe, and then dragged the tip of his tongue along the edge of her jaw.

She sucked in a breath and bucked against him. When that didn't move him, she tried a different tactic. "Let me go, Laurent," she said softly, sweetly.

"So now you use my name." How wonderful it sounded on her tongue. After all these years, it was a balm to his soul. A soul he'd thought was long gone, forsaken. He looked down at her, noticed that her eyes were an odd mixture of blue and silver. Ducking his head, he kissed her throat, her collarbone.

"Mine," he groaned against the tender skin between her breasts.

"Over my dead body."

He was momentarily distracted by the delicious mounds of flesh beneath him, and she twisted and pushed against him until she was free. He grabbed her foot and yanked her back across the bed.

He came down hard against her back. She fought like a Pit Bull, her fingernails shredding the bedding.

"You're already dead," he said. "Remember?"

"Not all of me." A sharp elbow connected with his ribs, and he howled in pain and rolled away from her.

Damn it to hell, she was strong.

Still, he reached for her. Her nails sliced his skin like a paper shredder. He grabbed her throat, and surprise flickered in her eyes. Then her shin connected with his balls, and he saw stars.

"You're…not gonna kill me," he puffed out, glaring at her. "So you might as well…give up."

"Never." She rubbed her throat. "I always complete the job."

"Listen, honey, my *were* is about two seconds away from making his debut, and we both know who always wins those fights. So do yourself a favor and keep your pretty skin intact."

"Your balls still hurting, big boy?" Her foot came at him again, but this time he was faster. He caught her foot in midair and gave it a hard twist. She spun through the air. He barely managed to duck out of the way of her other foot before she landed on the floor.

A quick roll, then a fancy flip had her standing upright again.

"Watch a lot of kung fu movies?" he asked as he pounced on her.

She hissed.

He snarled, and they both fought for the upper hand. Her back hit the wall, and he leaned in close. This wasn't how he'd envisioned getting his hands on her. In fact, it was the farthest thing from it. He'd never touched her in anger before. Never seen her angry. But she was out for blood this time. *His* blood.

She tensed her muscles and pushed against his chest. "You're not a half bad opponent."

"I'd have to say the same about you," he uttered, and deftly kissed her nose.

With a grunt, she shoved him away.

He grinned. "Cat and mouse. Is that how you like to play?"

"You make a nice mouse," she said, leaping over the bed and grabbing her sword.

He waited for her to come at him, knowing he could sidestep her moves all night. Would she ever grow tired of this game? Wasn't she ready to give in and let them both have the pleasure they desired? She started toward him, each step carefully placed on the floor. Lightning glinted off the sword at her side, its tip pointed at his chest.

He jumped left, then right, to avoid the blade. "When did you learn to fight?"

"Years ago." Wood cracked and splintered as she chopped into a table. He continued dodging her. She kept swinging. "Why. Won't. You. Die?" She punctuated each word with a jab.

"So this is your job? Killing people?" He rolled backwards over the bed, feeling like a playful, eight week-old pup. Her eyes flashed silver. He wasn't particularly afraid of her—and if he could take a time out, he was sure he'd laugh at the whole situation.

The woman he loved more than life itself had been hired to assassinate him, and here she was dancing around him in her lingerie, trying to slice him to bits. Yes, the Fates had a brutal sense of humor.

"Why are you not afraid of me?" She stopped to look at him. Her heaving breasts threatened to spill over the top of the lacey cups of her bra. Standing in the doorway, with rain splattering her feet, she was a vision. Lithe, toned, and delicious.

"I used to kill your kind for a living." He cocked his head to the side, watching her through his lashes as his words sank in.

She let out a piercing battle cry and leapt at him. He caught her wrists and held them high over her head.

"I *will* kill you," she promised. Her features hardened, and her tone was filled with fury.

"I'm not afraid of death."

Her eyebrows drew together and frowned as if she hadn't understood him. That glossy hair he longed to run his fingers through trailed over her shoulder in a way he found far too alluring for their present situation.

"My turn," he said. "Why do you kill?"

"Because it's what I was trained to do."

"You aren't very good at it."

She moved so quickly he hardly had time to react. Her blade sliced into his arm, and he growled low in his throat as he spun out of the way.

"Then again, I'm not used to fighting a mere woman. Perhaps women are not made to fight. To kill."

"Would you like to see my kill book?" Her fangs peeked over her lips again.

"Not particularly."

When she swung this time, he kicked the sword out of her hand. She hissed like a cat who'd just had its tail stepped on.

"Perhaps your heart just isn't in it." He gave her a dark, lingering look. And before she could reply, turned and walked out onto the balcony.

Rain poured down upon him, drenching his jeans and soaking his hair. Through the thick precipitation, he could make out a few landmarks and skyscrapers. They were on the top floor of a building. The balcony stretched left and right. The thunderstorm carried the salty scent of the ocean and put on a great light show.

A sharp pain seared his back.

"You're stupid to turn your back on me, *wolf*," she said, her voice raised above the roar of falling water.

"I told you—I'm not afraid of death."

The point of her sword moved to the base of his neck. A chill broke out over his skin. The feeling…couldn't be fear. He'd thought about it for so long; had welcomed it on more than one occasion. All this time, he'd thought that she, Violet, was dead.

Life had seemed so dim. It hadn't mattered how many women had graced his bed. How many parties he'd attended, or how much money he'd made. Travel, food, and life itself had become tasteless and boring. Death would take away the pain. The monotony.

Slowly, he turned to face her. Her hair was plastered against her porcelain skin, and her eyes had turned that weird shade of blue and silver. Water dripped from her nose and ran like a river between her breasts, disappearing beneath the lacey edge of her panties.

"Who hired you?" The tip of her weapon was only inches away from his throat, and he was completely vulnerable. A rare feeling.

She frowned. "Why do you care?"

"Don't you think a dying man deserves to know who paid for his execution?"

"I don't know the person's name."

"You lie."

She remained silent as the wind picked up, driving the rain into his skin like BB pellets. She seemed unaffected by the sharp, stinging sensation. Her face remained placid, as if she'd done this, had stood in front of a man ready to carry out his death, a thousand times.

Perhaps she had.

"Well, Violet, I have nothing left to live for." He knelt in front of her, wondering if she'd go through with it. Perhaps he should call his brother and cousins. But he did not want them to think him a coward. Resigned, yes.

With that little piece of hope inside him dead, he had nothing left on which to cling. Everything—his life, their future, was in her hands.

5

Laurent stared up into Cayenne's beautiful face. She blinked raindrops from her lashes and raised the sword.

"If you'd like to know who you are—" His words stopped her. "All you have to do is take my blood. All my memories of you are there. Of your childhood. The day you disappeared."

"Damn it, get up and fight like a man!"

"I have nothing left to fight for, sweetheart." He stared at her for a long moment, a resigned look in his eye. Then he gave her a lopsided smile. "Will you do me a favor?"

"What?" She bit out the word, almost shouted it.

"Smile."

"I—" She frowned.

He raised his eyebrows and sat back on his heels.

"I don't smile."

"Should I tickle you?" he asked. Thunder drowned out his voice.

How could he have a sense of humor at a time like this? Cayenne squared her shoulders and tried not to shiver in the cool rain.

Her resolve weakened. He was unlike anyone she'd ever met.

"Why is it so important to you?"

And for the first time she could remember, looking down at his handsome, water drenched face, she wanted to smile. If for no other reason, than because he was an interesting and unexpected adversary.

At some point in their battle he'd busted his lip. The wind changed, driving the rain at him. The small trickle of blood washed down his chin. He was so handsome. So…male. Proud. Even looking death in the eye.

"I'm a simple man, with simple desires. The one thing I wanted above all others was you.

"You were everything to me. A balm to my soul. A lighthouse in a stormy sea." His gaze was far off as he spoke. "Your smile quieted the beast threatening to take over. You were the one person in the world not pushing me to do what they wanted. What was expected.

"I would have done anything to make you laugh." He smiled, as if remembering her laughter. "I was besotted by a beautiful young woman who put everything into perspective. And I lost her."

His gaze met hers. "I lost you."

She bit her bottom lip, trying to remain emotionless.

"My happiness was stolen from me and along with it my dreams and my simple pleasures. Just as your happiness was stolen from you."

Something she'd never felt before filled her. Something unwelcome. All her life, she'd trained to be strong. To live in the moment. Always moving forward, never dwelling on the past. But she could remember the faces of every person she'd ever killed. Was Laurent right? Why hadn't she killed him when she'd had the opportunity? Was she losing her edge?

Another bolt of lightning crackled across the sky, and the wind shifted. He grinned at her. If she were the type to swoon, he'd have her falling at his feet.

"Do you always take this long to kill people?"

"Smart ass," she said.

The corner of his handsome mouth twitched, and something deep inside her stirred. She recognized the desire warring with her pity for killing this man. But she had no choice. It was the job she was hired to do. She didn't fail. She was trained *not* to fail.

"How much are you getting paid to kill me?"

"Why? Are you going to offer me double?"

This was the point when most of the evil men she'd killed bargained for their lives. She'd heard it all before. Money? How much? A car? Any kind she wanted. Houses on the four corners of the earth. Jewelry most women wouldn't dream of owning. Titles. Stocks. Dogs. Horses. Anything she wanted, if only she'd spare their lives. But the one thing she truly wanted, none of them could give.

"No." Laurent's voice was firm. Calm. Resigned. So he really didn't fear death. How odd. She was sure that once upon a time, before she'd become…*this*, she would've been terrified of finding herself at death's door. But now she walked in eternal, forsaken darkness. Unable to die a normal death or live a normal life. Unable to remember her past, before she'd become this machine. Unable to feel…

No. That was no longer true. She *did* feel. She experienced something when she looked into Laurent's face. Something she didn't dare name.

"Seriously. I have no desire to fight you. I never had any desire to fight. But I was good at it. I've handled too many weapons. Taken too many lives. When all I wanted was to end my own. So…" He pegged her with a gaze so intense she felt it all the way to her toes. "If you say you are not Violet and you're willing to dispatch my life, I'm ready to join her.

"My life is in your hands."

A full second ticked by and then her body took over as if it had a mind of its own. Her hand opened and the sword fell through the air and clattered against the concrete. She dropped to her knees in front of him, watching the trail of blood running from his lip.

Unsure of herself but driven by the need to touch him, she slid her hands over his corded biceps and up to his shoulders. He felt like rock covered in skin. Perfectly sculpted. Her gaze locked with his, and she saw questions there. But he remained silent.

Wordlessly, she leaned forward and touched her lips to his. Once, twice. She explored him slowly, watching him watch her as she did so. He didn't blink. She wasn't even sure he was still breathing.

At the corner of his mouth, her tongue snaked out and licked the cut.

He sucked in a sharp breath and clamped his arms around her waist. He didn't know his own strength as he crushed her to him. Even though her bones groaned in protest, he obviously realized she wasn't a tender little thing who needed to be handled gently. And although she knew she shouldn't enjoy the feel of his arms around her, she did.

Before she knew it was happening, he'd pulled her down on top of him. He slid his tongue inside her mouth, and his hands roamed her back.

Her eyes drifted closed, and she kissed him back like she'd always dreamed of kissing him. He was just as hot and hard as she'd imagined he would be. But there was a gentleness in him too, one she hadn't expected and couldn't explain.

Their mouths met and mated, over and over. The rain threatened to drown them. He nipped at her lips, teasing and coaxing her. How was she going to find the strength to pull away?

"Don't," he said, quickly switching their positions.

Her shoulder blades connected with cold, hard concrete, and she gasped. He snagged the fabric of her bra and ripped it away. When he looked down at her, awe filled his face. He slid his hands over her ribcage, the water slickening her skin, providing no resistance.

He cupped her breasts, his heat chasing away the chill that invaded her body, and she lost her will to fight. Gently, he kneaded her flesh. His face softened as he touched her. She sighed as his fingers brushed over her hardened nipples. Silently, she willed him to play with them. To bring her the pleasure he'd brought her in her dreams.

He stared straight into her eyes and flicked his thumbs back and forth, teasing her pebbled peaks.

A moan of ecstasy slid past her lips as he leaned down and took one of the aching peaks into his mouth. She wrapped her arms around his neck and held him to her.

His teeth nibbled the tender flesh, and she hissed out a breath. He laved her skin with his tongue, then took hold of her with gentle suction. Pleasure radiated through her, and she desperately wanted more.

He chuckled when that single thought escaped her lips. But like a good wolf, he moved to her other breast and lavished his attention on it.

She writhed beneath him, needing more.

Needing *him*.

The realization hit her like a door slamming in her face. She needed him. Wanted to feel him inside her. Needed to be one with this man.

Now.

She shouldn't want him, shouldn't need him. She shouldn't have this delicious ache between her legs, which only he could ease. But that didn't stop her.

"Why aren't you naked yet?" she demanded, trying to sound her sassiest even though she was petrified he'd notice the change in her.

"Do you want me naked?" he teased. The vibration of his voice hit the tender peak like a lightning bolt and zinged straight to her core.

"Yes. *Now.*" She arched her back and pressed herself against him.

A rich laughter rumbled from him an instant before he pulled away and shrugged out of his wet shirt. Then, with a naughty gleam in his eyes, shucked his jeans. She'd seen his hard muscled thighs in her dreams. But nothing could have prepared her for the glory of his cock. Long, thick, and as hard as a steal pipe.

He knelt between her legs and gave her panties a disapproving look before hooking his thumbs under them and tearing the flimsy garment from her body. His movements were quick, urgent.

"That's better," he said darkly.

Then he was on her, his arms bracketed around her, holding his weight. He nestled his hard length between her legs, and she immediately wrapped them around his hips. She was so ready for this. It was the oddest feeling. Like she'd been waiting for this forever.

"Hurry."

"Can't rush progress, sweetheart."

"Fuck me, already."

He stilled above her, shock filling his eyes. Then he shifted his weight and reached between them. She kissed his neck and shoulders, her hands urging him on. He tested her wetness, and her hips jerked.

"Inside me. Now!"

"You're a bossy little thing," he said, pulling his hand back. She rocked against him, trying to wrap herself around him.

She couldn't tell him about the crazy, mind

bending need that now claimed her. About the dreams that left her breathless and wanting. "No. I'm a horny little thing."

His lips found hers and she kissed him roughly, wrapping her arms around his neck. His tongue speared into her mouth, and he pushed his cock home. He was big and thick. The tiniest hint of pain pricked her as her body stretched to accommodate him. But she loved the feeling. It was real. True. For the first time in a very long time, she felt alive.

Just what she'd feared—and had prayed would happen.

A perfect fit. Laurent had always known it would be the case between him and Violet. Deep down, he'd always known they were created for each other. With her, he was sure he could have made a life, enjoyed his life. Or at least, the time he'd been given. After she'd disappeared...

No, he wouldn't think about it. She was here now. Squirming beneath him. Thrusting her hips against his.

She scratched his back and urged him on with breathy little words in French. He braced his arms around her slender frame and made love to her in earnest. Silently, he stared into her brilliant blue eyes. Eyes he'd missed so much. He let his body say the words.

Then he asked, "Am I hurting you?"

"No!" she cried, tightening her legs around his back. "Keep going."

"Gladly, *petite*." He couldn't stop now. He thrust into her tight little glove until she came apart beneath him. Her screams filled his ears. She tightened her arms and legs around him, and her sheath gripped his cock, giving it one hell of a massage.

He couldn't hold back. Didn't want to. So he let himself go and groaned in her ear as he came. He relished the feel of her body as it went from tight-as-a-bow to soft-and-spent.

He lay there for a few moments, savoring the bliss. Memorizing the feel of her. Savoring her scent.

"Thank the gods," she murmured, nestling her cheek against his.

"Enjoy yourself?" The smug part of him wanted her to tell him how fabulous she thought he was, how wonderful she felt. After everything between them, both new and old, he wanted her resistance gone.

"Very much." She sounded sated and sleepy. That worked for him. He wouldn't mind spending the rest of the night on top of her and having her wrapped around him.

Slowly, however, against his cock's wishes, he pulled out of her body and stared down at the beautiful woman lying in the rain. She was strong, sure, and sexy as hell.

She gave him a sultry smile that made his cock twitch.

Feeling decidedly possessive, he picked her up and carried her into the bathroom adjoining the bedroom. He wanted to dry her off, but she reached into the shower and turned on the water.

"Next, I suppose you'll want me to soap your back," he said as he nuzzled her neck. She made no move to get out of his arms. In fact, her body seemed almost relaxed.

"Or something else."

"Are you flirting with me, little vamp?" His wolf howled with happiness.

"Could be."

He stepped into the shower and slowly let her down to stand on her own two feet. Warm water cascaded over them, and she pressed herself against him from shoulder to knee.

"I've never done it in a shower before."

Her words made him hard again in a heartbeat. She reached between them and wrapped her hand around his dick.

I'm right, he thought, as he let himself be seduced. *A perfect fit.*

6

Cayenne woke with a burning pain in her chest. She clutched a hand over her heart and sat up in bed. Outside, the rain had stopped and darkness held the city in its clutches. She glanced down and saw a tattoo-like mark peeking through her fingers. Fearing the worst she lifted her hand. Three linked circles. She squeezed her eyes shut, hoping she was dreaming.

Okay, don't panic. Right. Easier said than done. She dared another look. Still there. Definitely not dreaming. She sucked in a shuddering breath.

This was not good. How had she let herself be seduced by him? Glancing over her shoulder she stared at the handsome sleep tousled man next to her and had her answer. Sexy laugh lines bracketed his handsome mouth. She nibbled her bottom lip to keep from leaning over and planting her lips against his. No. This was definitely not good.

He looked so peaceful there against the satiny-soft sheets. Too peaceful. Too perfect. Perfect for her.

Frustrated, she slipped from the bed. What the hell had she been thinking? He was…no…is the target!

Where was her bra? She spotted the remaining shreds of fabric lying in a soggy heap on the balcony.

Failure was not an option. That singular thought had been engrained in her. So what had she been thinking?

How had she allowed herself to be seduced by a Cajun werewolf?

She'd had the chance to do her job but she'd been the one to drop her sword and kneel before him. She'd own that the fault was her own. But somehow…it didn't feel like a fault. Not when she'd been in his arms, kissing his lips.

For just a moment she'd been Cayenne the woman, not Cayenne the assassin. For but a moment she'd been able to glimpse a different future. One where she had a handsome, spine-tingling man in her life who murmured endearments and pleasured her until she couldn't walk.

Longing filled her as she bent to retrieve fresh clothes. Over the years she'd wondered what it would be like to live a normal life. But she never allowed herself to dwell on those thoughts for long. Until she'd earned back her freedom from Madame, there was no point in daydreaming about the future.

The sun would be up soon and if she hurried she could make her escape before Laurent even knew she was gone. And once she was on the road, with plenty of distance between them, she'd figure out what to tell Madame about her failure. Just thinking the word left a sour taste in her mouth. She'd never failed before. Maybe she could lie and say the job was done. Who would know?

Besides the client.

Okay, so she wouldn't return to Madame at all. She was one job away from completion and therefore her contract wasn't exactly fulfilled, but hadn't she done enough?

Cayenne looked out at the city. Ninety-nine good kills. Did she have the courage to just walk away? Disappear? Go rogue?

She sneered at herself, despising her weakness and self doubt. Cayenne Laroque was a master assassin not a pawn on someone else's chess board. She shouldn't have to answer to anyone. Why had it taken her so long to figure that out?

Why had she held on to that misguided sense of loyalty? Why had it taken meeting Laurent before she'd been willing to change?

Cayenne smiled, mind made up. Peace

washed over her. She could make it on her own. Set her own fees. Take jobs she believed in. Take control of her destiny. Of course, she'd be on the run but—

A knock at the door disturbed the quiet and her runaway thoughts. She reached for her dagger and sent up a mind block to protect herself from whomever waited on the other side. After slipping a tank top over her head, she closed the bedroom door behind her. Measured steps carried her across the small living area, and she took up a defensive position as she cracked open the front door.

Emil.

How had he found her again? She pursed her lips together to keep from sneering.

"Cayenne, my dear, I heard of your latest conquest. Is the job done?" How had he heard? Contracts we're supposed to be private.

She studied him closely. His jet black hair, piercing blue eyes and chiseled features made women fall at his feet. But she would never trust a man more beautiful than she.

Hardly anything was handsome about him to her now. He was tall and lean, with features so refined they were sharp. His cheeks were hollow…just like his soul. And his eyes, as lively as death warmed over.

Today, he was dressed in an edgy suit of charcoal gray. His shirt and tie were the same color as his jacket, and she wondered briefly what it would take to put a scar on his pretty face.

But vampires didn't scar. They fought, they bled, and they healed. But they never scarred. Unless one counted the scars on the inside. Not that she had anything left on the inside that would ever need healing.

"I always do the job I'm sent to do," she quipped and started to close the door.

His hand shot out, holding it open.

"Excellent." Then, he clasped his arms behind his back and rocked back on his heels before taking a step forward. "I thought perhaps you might invite me in. We have much to discuss."

She hated the way he looked down his nose at her as if he were so superior and she'd mindlessly do his bidding. Early on, she'd learned the truth of his background. He hadn't been an aristocrat when he was alive. He wasn't highborn and he'd stolen most of his wealth. Gambling was just one of the many vices he'd accumulated since she'd known him. A long string of prostitutes who'd graced his bed over the years was another.

As usual, he deluded himself. Eleven years with not a peep and here he was knocking on her door again. He reminded her of a lovesick teenager.

"Perhaps I won't." She kept her foot firmly planted at the base of the door. In the years since he'd turned her, she'd caught on to his ways, seen the lust in his eyes. She'd grown strong. And resentful. It was one of the few emotions she allowed herself.

"Cayenne—"

"Save it, Emil. Go back to wherever you came from and suck on someone else for a change."

"How can you speak to me like that? After I saved you!" This was the same broken record she'd heard before. Always trying to guilt her.

He leaned in close, a deep frown marring his face. His nostrils flared. "Dieu, Cayenne. What have you done?" He gasped as if she'd struck him. Her lips curved upward at the thought.

"Done?"

He leaned back a fraction and she raised a brow. "You smell just like that—that dog." He sneered and his nose squished up in disgust.

"Who I sleep with is none of your business."

"Actually, it's very much my business." He paused. Cayenne remained silent. If he was waiting for her to ask why he'd wait forever. A smug expression graced his lips and lit his eyes. "I bought your contract from Madame."

She remained silent. Unaffected. In those early days with Madame she'd felt thankful to the woman for bringing Cayenne back to health. But somewhere along the way she'd lost her gratitude, her respect and her patience. She felt even less for Emil.

But Cayenne had already decided enough was

enough. It was time to close the door on that chapter of her life. She gripped the dagger tighter and ran her tongue over her fangs. Did she dare wipe that look of satisfaction off his face?

"You're mine, dearest."

She spoke slowly, enunciating each word carefully. Power rippled through her. "I am not your dearest."

"Of course you are darling. Now let me in so we can talk."

"Over my dead body."

"That can be arranged!" His hand shot through the open door and grabbed her by the throat. But in a lightning fast move of her own, she flicked her dagger, angling it against his groin.

He stilled and his eyes went wide. It was almost comedic but she didn't laugh. She savored the power she held over him.

"I spent years in training to become the best warrior Madame's academy has ever seen. What makes you think that you're man enough to take me?"

His eyes went dark, stormy as he squeezed her throat. *Never panic*, she heard Madame's words in her mind. Cayenne cocked her head to the side, watching him closely, and pressed the blade closer to his flesh.

"Let me go or I will take you apart piece by piece."

He stared at her for a long moment and must

have ultimately decided she was deadly serious. He dropped his hand and stepped back.

"Let's get something straight. I am not your pawn, nor am I your property."

"No, you're a whore. A whore who fucks dogs." He glanced past her and then took another step back.

"It takes one to know one."

"This isn't over Cayenne. I made you. I can destroy you."

She laughed. "You and what army?"

He paused then, eyes narrowed, as if trying to decide if she were bluffing or not. She wasn't. And they both knew he was no match for her.

He stuttered. Huffed. Puffed up like a blow fish. Then he gave her a final dark look before spinning on his heal and stalking the short distance to the elevator. *That's right. Go on. Don't want to draw attention to yourself.*

She waited until he'd stepped on and the numbers over head began descending before she shut the door and locked every lock.

Dealing with Emil always zapped her energy. Her hand went to her neck. Had he really thought he could scare her? She'd never been afraid of him.

Kill him. The thought was appealing. But could she really kill one of her own kind, much less her sire?

. . .

Emil stared at his reflection in the elevator doors. Insolent girl. She tested him far too often. And she'd given herself to that—that beast.

Not that he hadn't gone slumming in his day. But he'd always thought her above that. A rare beauty. His Cayenne was as strong willed as they came.

Independent or not, he was tired of waiting for her to come to her senses. He was tired of feeling like a pathetic boy, begging for her affections. He'd made the mistake of letting her escape him all those years ago. He knew now he should have bound more than her memories.

"Cayenne…Cayenne," he muttered and pulled out his cell phone. When the doors opened, he stepped into the lobby and pressed the first number on his call list.

"I need you here. Now."

Laurent roused slowly and reached out to the woman next to him, but his hand only touched air. His eyelids snapped open, and fear knotted his stomach. He glanced at the empty spot where Cayenne had slept next to him. Raking his hands down his face, he pondered the great cosmic joke that was his love life. Two hundred plus years of loving the same woman. A ghost.

A ghost who'd been very much flesh and

blood last night. Who'd let him inside her body. Over and over again.

Vivid images flashed through his mind. His lips on her stomach. Her mouth parted in an O as she came apart beneath him. Their hands, with her long fingernails, entwined.

Outside, the sounds from the city below drifted up to their window. The steady purr of a zipper drew his attention, and he pushed himself into a sitting position. The object of his thoughts sat on the other side of the room in a chair. His heart leapt into his throat when he realized she was getting dressed.

"What are you doing?" he asked, although it was obvious. "Why?"

Her delicate brow rose, and she gave him a *what does it look like I'm doing?* look as she zipped her boots. Gone was the woman who'd been so playful last night, and in her place was a woman determined to leave him.

"I must go."

His heart ached over his years of loss, but watching her gather her things now…now that he'd found her again, it was like a dagger to the gut. Not ready to be discarded a second time, his wolf demanded he claim her. He couldn't lose her again. He couldn't. *Wouldn't.* He wasn't going to live another two hundred years wondering if she were alive. Wondering where she was, and what the hell to do with his sorry self without her.

"Damn it, why?" he asked again.

She lifted a brow. "Did you think I'd just stay in bed with you?"

"After last night? Hell, yes. Don't tell me you didn't feel it too, because I know you did." They'd connected on a whole different level.

She stood and slipped her long, lean arms into the sleeves of her coat, tugged the lapels together, and turned away. Something about her movements seemed unnatural, like she was hiding something.

What the hell had happened after he'd fallen asleep? He swung his feet to the floor and stalked toward her. As his hands closed around her hips and spun her around, a tiny gasp left her mouth.

He took full advantage, locking his lips onto hers. Searching, speaking. Telling her everything he couldn't put into words. Things he was too scared to say aloud.

At first she was still, uninvolved. But when his tongue teased its way past her lips, she came alive in his arms, shifted her hips against his, and gripped his upper arms. The leather of her coat was cool beneath his hands, but he craved her soft skin and the warmth they ignited together.

When she tipped her head back, he trailed kisses down her jaw. She pressed herself against him from chest to knee. *Not close enough.*

Pushing the jacket out of the way, he curved his hands over her hips and pulled her hard against his growing erection. Soft mews came from her lips, and he nibbled the tender skin of her neck.

Opening his eyes, he took her in, the body he'd seen for so many years and yet, had only now begun to know. The woman who'd changed so much from the girl he'd once loved. He could feast his eyes on her for days.

As if realizing he'd stopped kissing her and was looking his fill, she opened her eyes. He wanted to laugh at the look of embarrassment on her pretty face, but she turned away.

He gripped her shoulders and turned her back. She pressed her hand over her heart, but not quickly enough to hide the mark that now lay on her skin.

He looked down at his own chest, and his heart expanded with happiness.

"We're mated." He tried to keep his voice even, because he wasn't sure how she was going to take the news. And if trying to hide the mark were any indication...

She opened her mouth to speak but closed it again when heavy footsteps echoed through the streets below their room. Laurent let her go and moved to the balcony, peering over the railing.

"Okay, who else did you piss off last night?" he asked, coming back into the room. She looked past him to the warm glow of early morning light.

"I told you I had to go," she said, hands on her hips. *Men never listen…*

Laurent glanced around for his clothes. "Do all your friends dress in black and carry automatic weapons?" he asked, shrugging into his shirt, then he pulled his pants over his lean hips.

Automatic weapons? That sounded like Emil's goons. She rolled her eyes. "I wouldn't call them my friends." The delicious hum of adrenaline tightened her muscles. She doubled checked her pack and slung it over her shoulder.

"What would you call them?" Hopping up and down, he put on his loafers. She smiled at his ironic choice of footwear.

But if they were indeed Emil's men, as she was sure they were, he obviously wasn't taking no for an answer this time. And he was obviously too stupid to take their fight out of the city. Away from prying eyes and innocent bystanders. Worst of all, the slimy weasel wasn't man enough to face her himself. He probably figured if he ambushed her they could take her by force and she'd coerced into submitting.

Never before had she felt so divided. She'd always fought her battles by herself. But coming down from an orgasmic high, she really didn't have the energy to take on Emil and his men. Her training warred with her sense of self preservation. Part of her wanted to stay and fight…but another part wanted to run and hide.

"I'd call them *enemies*," she said, craning her head to listen. Four, maybe five men were coming up the emergency staircase. The elevator would have been a much quieter point of entry.

Looking at Laurent now…she took a deep, sobering breath and admitted to herself that she wanted more than the life she'd been trained for. If she had the chance to control her destiny, didn't that mean she could live the life she wanted, apart from death dealing?

She wasn't sure she'd be good at anything else, but she had plenty of money to live and endless time to discover a new talent. And she could always fall back on her sword.

Laurent stared down at her and she stared right back. She wanted a chance to start over. To disappear. And she needed to feed. Her gaze zeroed in on Laurent's neck. She licked her lips.

"So what do you say? Stay and fight or run away with me and start over?"

"I don't run away," she said automatically. The sentiment had been drilled into her.

He stopped in front of her. "Didn't they teach you that sometimes the smartest move in battle is to retreat?"

"No."

"Come with me. We can disappear together." Smiling as if he had all the confidence in the world, he held out his hand. She leaned down, revealing a luscious swell of skin, and tucked a dagger into her boot.

The footsteps in the stairwell grew louder. She glanced from him to the door and back. The moment stretched on and he tried to read her mind but her thoughts were rapid fire pistons.

"Alright," she said, sounding breathless. The single word was music to his ears. She stared at his hand for half of a second before taking it.

He kissed her and then left her to push the dresser in front of the door.

"What are you doing? That's our way out."

"There's another way."

Her gaze swerved to the balcony. "Are you suggesting we make a rope out of the bed linens and shimmy our way down?"

Parts of him stirred at the thought of her luscious behind shimmying. "I'd love to watch you shimmy…some other time."

He glanced out at the rapidly rising sun. "How do you feel about sunlight?"

"Sunlight?" The word was quick and shrill. Had there not been men after them, he would have taken a moment to enjoy how comical her expression was.

Instead, he nodded grimly. He'd heard that vamps had become immune to sunlight but he didn't want to test it on her. The roof really was the best way out since he had no idea who was after her or if they'd shoot first and ask questions later.

"I prefer to stay out of it unless I'm wearing SPF 50."

He wrapped her jacket around her and cinched the belt tight. It came down well over the tops of her boots. But her hands and face were bare. "Let's go."

"Great," she said with a grumble. But she sheathed her weapon and started after him. He lead the way to the balcony and down to the end of the building. Behind them, the door to her suite crashed open. Gunfire ricocheted through the room. His heartbeat quickened along with his footsteps.

They were on the top floor, and he quickly gaged the distance to the roof line. Sometimes being super strong came in handy. *Now* was one of those times.

He let go of her hand and pointed a finger to the roof above. "Up you go."

"You're joking." She glanced down at his finger and then up at the rooftop.

"Nope." He grabbed her around the waist from behind and, as gently as possible, hurtled them both to the roof. Voices from below drove him forward.

The tarred pebbles crushed beneath their feet as they ran across the expanse. When they reached the edge, he surveyed her hands and face.

Her skin was turning pink far too fast for his liking.

An alley stretched between the buildings, and she looked at him with an arched brow. Effortlessly, she stepped onto the ledge, lifted her arms, and soared through the air with a grace he had to admire. She landed easily on the other side and turned to look at him.

Wasting no time, he leapt after her, and they took off running again. He didn't dare look back. Pushing ahead was their only option. Right now, he didn't care who was after them, or why. But he very much wanted to stay alive.

When they came to the side of the building, Cayenne put her hand on its edge and soared over it as if it were a vaulting horse. The fire escape groaned under their weight as he joined her. Rusted metal flaked off as they descended.

"Do you see them?" she asked when they were almost to the bottom.

"No. But they've probably got this place staked out." That was a professional operation if he'd ever seen one.

She dropped to the pavement next to him and pushed her hair out of her face.

"You read my mind. There's a car park on the next block," she said, and he admired that she had an exit strategy. Side by side, they raced down the sidewalk and into the concrete parking deck, up a flight of stairs and along a row of cars.

. . .

Emil hissed as he watched his prey racing down the street with the werewolf. He should have killed them both when he'd had the chance. Biting back a curse he spun on his heel and confronted his men.

Find her. Kill him.

The wolf had to live somewhere close by. As for Cayenne, Emil wouldn't rest until he had his fangs in that beautiful neck of hers.

7

Cayenne strutted over to a shiny black Audi, and Laurent forced his gaze away from her swinging hips. Pulling out her sword, she tightened her grip and smashed the hilt into the small window behind the driver's door. A siren blared through the tight space. Wasting no time, she reached into the car, and unlocked the door. Tossing her sword inside, she dove beneath the dashboard and, a second later, the alarm fell silent.

He lifted his eyebrows. Where had she learned to do that?

"Never mind where," she said. "Get in."

Laurent fell into the cushy leather passenger seat. "Head north. My family has an estate where we'll be safe there while we figure out where to go."

"I know."

That's right. She'd been tracking him. Hunting him. Watching him like a deer at the end of her scope.

"Emil will track us," she said. Who the hell was this Emil bastard? And what did he mean to her?

"Then it will be the last mistake he ever makes."

"You don't know Emil."

"You don't know my family."

"I don't know family, *period.*" She pulled onto the road and shifted the stick smoothly. In and out of traffic she weaved, confidant in her ability to change lanes.

"How's your skin?" he asked.

"It itches. But at least it doesn't burn."

He wanted to fix it. Sooth it. Something. But he doubted she'd let him, so he put on his seatbelt and watched to make sure they weren't being followed.

He also didn't tell her the real reason he wanted to get her back to the Deveraux estate. She'd find out soon enough with the way she was driving.

After they turned off the road and pulled up to the gate of Sebastian's estate, he reached across her and pushed the button to lower her window.

"Press the call button," he instructed.

"Fancy."

"My cousin's popular. Keeps the scavengers at

bay." But evidently it hadn't kept *her* at bay. She seemed to be intimately familiar with him and his schedule. He'd have to talk to Sebastian about beefing up security again.

"Yeah?" came a voice from the call box.

"Jules? It's Laurent. Let me in."

"Who's that with you?"

"You wouldn't believe me if I told you." He knew they'd had cameras installed, but figured his cousin probably couldn't make out Cayenne's features.

The gates rumbled open, and she eased the car forward. At the end of the long gravel drive sat an Antebellum home with a wide wrap-around porch. Tall trees framed it, offering shade in the summer heat.

She slowed the car to a stop in the circular drive, and Laurent quickly opened his door. He scanned the driveway and then the road as far as he could see.

"Nice car, cousin," Jules said from the front porch.

"Thanks."

Cayenne got out and turned toward his cousin.

"Holy shit."

Sebastian stepped out onto the porch next to Jules and narrowed his gaze. He held Amanda close to his side. "Violet?"

"Why does everyone keep calling me that?" Cayenne asked.

"Let's go inside so we can talk." Laurent led the way. As Cayenne passed Sebastian, Laurent heard him suck in a deep breath.

"You're a vampire." He didn't sound pleased; not that Laurent expected him to welcome her with open arms. At one time they'd both fought vampires. Killed them in battle after bloody battle.

"Really? I thought the fangs were for show," she quipped. Laurent chuckled, loving this new sassy side of her . Hand against her lower back, he ushered her into the foyer. Her skin was red, like she had a painful sunburn.

"Does it hurt?"

"Of course it bloody hurts," she snapped.

He lifted a brow.

"I'll be fine in a few minutes," she murmured, her voice softening. She held herself rigid and swept the home's dim interior with her gaze, pausing on André who stood at the bottom of the stairs.

"Okay, explain. *Now.*" Sebastian's tone was dark and terse.

"This is Cayenne," Laurent said.

His cousin's dark brow inched upward.

"It's complicated," Laurent said and then turned his attention to André. "I need your help.

You once offered to bind my memories. Can you unbind hers?"

André stepped forward, regarding Cayenne closely. "Only the one who bound her can break the binding."

The breath Laurent had been holding woshed out of his lungs and he dropped his head.

"You brought me here so he could make me remember my past?" Cayenne asked, her blue gaze searing into him.

"I need you to remember. It's the only way you'll ever be free to make your own decisions."

"To choose you, you mean," she said softly. There was a long, uncomfortable pause.

Amanda and Angel shared a quizzical look. "Well, Laurent, Cayenne, I hope you're staying for supper."

"We need to go," Laurent said, hating the disappointment in Amanda's eyes.

"Why?" Amanda asked.

"Where?" Jules chimed in.

An excellent question. He heard Cayenne's thought as clearly as if she'd spoken aloud.

My brother has a cabin up North. We'll go there.

"Someone's after us," Laurent said.

"Me," Cayenne corrected. "They're after me."

"And me by association," Laurent countered, his hands clamped over his hips.

"Who?" Sebastian's mood seemed to be darkening by the second.

"Most likely, my Sire, Emil," Cayenne said. "And his cronies."

"Will the sun hold them?" Sebastian directed his question to Laurent.

"The young ones, yes. The older ones have developed an immunity over the years," Cayenne said, glancing down at her hands, her skin now a faint pink. Like werewolves, vampires had incredible healing abilities.

"Were you followed?"

"Not the way she drives," Laurent said with a smile he didn't feel.

He'd convinced her to come with him. To team up. But for how long? Just because they were mated didn't mean she had to stay with him. His gut was tied in knots.

Jules hadn't stopped staring at Cayenne since they'd stepped through the door.

"It's like seeing a ghost," he murmured.

"How did you find each other?" Sebastian asked.

"I was hired to kill him," she said wryly.

Amanda squeaked as Sebastian hustled both her and Angelica into the sitting room. Jules was in the air, headed for Cayenne's throat, before Laurent could blink. Laurent jerked Cayenne behind him and wrapped a hand around Jules neck.

"She's also my mate." He released his cousin with a shove.

"Your *mate?*" Sebastian demanded.

"I don't believe you," Jules added.

"She's a vampire!" Sebastian said, as if that settled everything.

Jules glared at him. "She was hired you kill you, you idiot."

Laurent jerked his shirt open to reveal the mating mark. His cousins fell silent. They stared at the mark, and he could see their jaws working. Jules finally backed up a step, his posture erect and ready for battle. Jealousy and defeat played over his face.

Amanda and Angelica were both human. Laurent knew Sebastian and Jules lamented that they could not share the immortal bond of mates. How the tables had turned in the last twenty four hours. Was it just yesterday that he'd been jealous of *their* relationships?

"I thought we let that whole killing me thing drop," Laurent whispered to Cayenne. She gave an apologetic shrug.

The two blondes emerged from the sitting room and glared at their men, then turned their gazes on Cayenne.

"You don't intend to kill him now, do you?" Amanda asked, falling into her role as the Alpha female of their pack. Cayenne shifted to stand next to him.

"If he dies, *I* die," she said dryly.

His mate was obviously not pleased with the reception she'd received. He looked down at her, saw the familiar face he'd long loved, and wished against hope she'd feel even an ounce of what he felt.

"But if that weren't the case..." Sebastian crossed his massive arms over his chest.

She look up at him, as if she were mulling it over. Laurent held his breath.

"I wouldn't harm him." Was the icy prison around her heart melting? He could only hope. "We should go. I don't want to put your family in danger."

"You already have," Sebastian said, his tone terse.

"Cousin…"

"You'll stay here. They could already be tracking your scent."

"Sebastian," Amanda said soothingly, her hand on her husband's arm.

His cousin paused long enough to look down at her. A look of love passed between them before his jaw hardened and he pegged Laurent and Cayenne with a glare.

"They've brought danger to our doorstep. The least they can do is help us defend it. Jules, watch the front. André, the back. Honey, call Burke."

Laurent wanted to argue. He wanted to leave, to disappear and have Cayenne all to himself.

Reading his thoughts again, Cayenne put her hand on his arm and shook her head. *He's right. If they're already tracking us, our best bet is to stay here. I'll take care of Emil when the time is right.*

Amanda turned to the phone on the entry table and started dialing.

"Come on. I need to know everything you know about Emil," Laurent said, taking Cayenne by the hand. He lead her into the sitting room. Amanda had redecorated it since she'd become Sebastian's wife. Large sofas upholstered in comfortable fabric sat across from each other. The fireplace at the other end of the room didn't get much use, so she'd placed a fern inside it. He hadn't given the living room much thought before, but seeing it with fresh eyes helped Laurent decide it was his favorite spot in the house. It was roomy and comfortable. The kind of place he yearned to have for himself.

A place where he could kick up his feet and hunker down at night. Where he could cuddle his woman at his side. The corners of his lips tugged upward.

"What are you smiling at?" she asked.

"Just thinking about you, *cheri*. Now, tell me about Emil. You said he'd find you."

She sat on the edge of one of the sofas with her knees and feet together. "He turned me. I don't remember when or where. Only after. He wouldn't tell me anything about my past. He told me I had great hands." She held her fingers out and studied the blood red nails.

"Great hands?"

She looked around as she talked, everything about her nonchalant. "He came on to me, and I slapped him. He told me I had good hands. Swift and sure. He gave me a sword. And everything felt…right. The weight. My grip on the handle."

Laurent realized this wasn't just the story of Emil. It was Cayenne's story as well. How she'd become who she was.

"So I ran away, taking the sword with me. He wanted me to join his little posse. Be his mistress. He's very…possessive. I knew that if I was going to get away from him I'd have to leave. Run away. Learn my way around a sword.

"I figured if I knew how to handle myself I could fend off his…affections. The first few years, I traveled a lot. It didn't take much for me to live back then. One night, I got in a fight with another vamp over a clock tower. Jean Claude was a brilliant swordsman. Before he was turned, he'd been a top crafter. He knew his weapon and his art. But by then, I'd become pretty handy myself. When he realized we were better matched than he'd thought, he offered to train me."

"So that's how you became…"

She shook her head. "I accepted. We trained each night. After a while, I fell in love with him."

Love? The word gave Laurent heartburn. All this time. He'd been pining over her, and she'd been falling in love with someone else. He stalked to the window and looked out.

"Hey, you wanted to hear my story."

"I wanted to hear about Emil."

"You will. When Emil found out about Jean Claude and me, he came back to Paris. I came home one night and found Jean Claude dead, with Emil's dagger beside his ashes. It was as good a message as any. A calling card to let me know he still considered me his property.

"I left and went to Asia. A group of werewolves did a number on me about a year after I arrived. Another trainer found me. Nursed me back to health. Everyone calls her Madame. She ran a school for people like me. Assassins. She was looking for women to bring into her dynasty. Men never suspect a beautiful woman, she said.

"At that point I was pretty lethal with a sword but there were plenty of other weapons to learn. Ways to defend myself or take down an opponent. She was an expert in tactics and everything else an assassin would need to know.

"I didn't have anything else to live for. And she'd given me shelter. Fed me. She made me a deal. And then she molded me into a soldier. Taught me things and trained me to kill. Over time, I grew immune to sunlight and took more jobs."

"How many?"

"You were to be my hundredth. And then I was to be released."

"Released?"

"To work for myself."

A high price to pay for training.

"I live well. She taught me that. But I'm her slave, a machine, until I earn my freedom. That was the deal."

Until she earned her boss enough money.

"And Emil," Laurent said. "Why not kill him?"

"The time was never right."

A rat-a-tat-tat on the door frame drew his attention, and Angelica's strawberry blond hair and big green eyes popped into view.

"Jambalaya's on the stove if you're hungry."

Laurent murmured his thanks and looked down at Cayenne. It was too much to take in. Did she feel loyalty to Emil for turning her all those years ago? And this other man, Jean Claude—did she still love him?

His stomach rumbled. "You skipped breakfast," she murmured.

Eating hadn't been on his radar since he'd first seen her standing in the middle of the street, rain showering down around her, looking like she'd just stepped from a painting.

"Go eat," she urged. "I'll keep watch."

She stepped to the window and looked out, cocking her head to the right.

His stomach rumbled again. He left her standing there and headed for the kitchen to eat.

Either the timing was never right, or she'd never had the heart to kill the one who'd created her. Who'd saved her from death. Only Cayenne knew the truth.

After lunch, footsteps sounded from the back of the house. Cayenne strode back into the foyer and looked out the windows flanking the door. She knew Emil would use the cover of night to attack. Young vamps could not stand direct sunlight.

The question was, how long would it take him to find her? And once he found her, would he attack immediately or wait until their guard was down?

"Jules, you and Laurent take first watch. I've got some calls to make," Sebastian's deep voice called from behind her.

Jules kissed Angelica, before sending her upstairs. Then he strode to the window and brushed aside the curtains.

After a long silent moment he spoke. "Laurent's waited a long time for you."

Her defenses went up. "His mistake," she said without thinking.

But that wasn't right. It wasn't Laurent's mistake. It was Emil's.

"For loving you that much?" Jules words were filled with malice. She wasn't surprised. She couldn't even blame him. Jules Deveraux loved his cousin. She admired that kind of loyalty. The only thing she was loyal to was her sword.

"You'd rather just believe love doesn't exist, wouldn't you?" he asked. "So you can go back to doing whatever it is you do."

"It's what I know." A painful but true admission. But it wasn't everything she was. She couldn't believe that anymore.

"It *was*," he corrected, almost as if he'd read her thoughts.

"What is it that you want?" she asked, halting right behind him. She had to admit that Jules Deveraux was a handsome man. He was tall and lean, with the same dark looks that Laurent was blessed with. She heard his heartbeat, strong and steady, and her fangs lengthened ever-so-slightly.

"Most people would die for the chance to be loved the way he loves you."

"I'm not most people." And she'd already died once. For what? What good had it done?

"No, you're not." He turned and looked down at her, his eyes holding a mixture of hate and pity. "You don't deserve him."

The words, sharp and true, cut her like a knife. She rocked back on her heels and frowned.

Then she turned and continued her trek across the wooden floor.

Jules was right. She hardly knew Laurent. Well, that wasn't exactly true. She'd watched him for the better part of two weeks, and had seen enough to form her own opinions. Learned enough to know what kind of man he truly was. Despite his moody exterior, that possessive streak, and the occasional fit of temper, he was a nice guy. Generous and charming.

"You're right. I don't deserve him." She stopped next to Jules and surveyed the yard. "But just for the record, I didn't ask for any of this."

"No, you didn't." He turned toward her. "But you wanted him all those years ago. I find it hard to believe you'd just throw all that away."

"I don't remember any of it."

"But you feel it."

How did he know that? She cocked her head and looked up at him.

"He cried for you."

Cayenne shook her head unable to believe his words. Not Laurent.

"He did." Jules turned her toward him. "He didn't function for more than a year. I think he's always mourned you."

"There's never been anyone else?"

He shook his head.

"I find that hard to believe," she lied. She didn't want to believe it. It made her feel guilty, and she'd never experienced that particular emotion before. At least not that she remembered.

"Well, believe it, Sister-Mate. You're the only woman he's ever wanted. And you don't know how damn lucky you are to be mated." A trace of sorrow touched his eyes, and she instantly wished she could give her bond to him and Angelica. They loved each other. Their connection was obvious. The way they looked at each other, so silly and lovestruck. They deserved to be mated.

Cayenne was attracted to Laurent, and the sex was great. But love? After seeing Sebastian and Amanda and Jules and Angel, she wasn't sure she'd know what love was if it smacked her upside the head.

"You know *I* don't share, cousin." Laurent's voice cut through the silence. Cayenne's stomach did a flip flop, and she stepped away from Jules.

"I don't either," Jules said.

"That's not what I hear."

"Okay. I think I've caused enough chaos for one day." Cayenne stepped between the two men, who were eying each other like a pair of dogs fighting over a bone. "Where's our room?"

8

Laurent backed away from Jules and took her hand. Silently, he lead her up the stairs and to the right. She could feel the emotions rolling off of him. So much had happened to him in less than twenty four hours. At the end of the hall, he opened a door on the left.

Cayenne stepped into the room and looked around at the masculine furnishings. A big bed with a simple, dark colored comforter claimed the center of the space; a large wooden dresser sat against the opposite wall; and a wingback chair in a complimentary fabric took up the corner next to the window. Not a bad place to camp for a while.

The door slammed behind her, and she whirled. "Camp for a while?" Laurent had a dangerous look in his eyes.

"If you don't like what you hear, stop reading my mind."

"We're mated," he said, stalking toward her. Cayenne crossed her arms over her chest and held her ground. She wasn't afraid of him. "So don't get any ideas about the other men in this house."

"Who says I'm interested in them? Don't let your jealousy think for you. What you saw was your cousin giving me the third degree, *imbecile*." She pointed her finger at his chest.

"You are *my* mate. Mine. Got that, *petite*?" He grabbed her upper arms.

You don't deserve him.

She focused on Jules words and gathered her courage as she put her hands on his shoulders and pushed him away. He didn't let go. "So you keep telling me." Her voice rose.

"I apparently haven't gotten it through that pretty little head of yours!"

"Just because we both have the same mark, doesn't mean we're meant to be."

Laurent looked as if she'd hit him. Or cut out his heart. And for the second time that night, she felt guilty. This was why Madame had taught her to block out her emotions. They sucked.

His gaze searched her face and she felt him reading her mind again. "I'll kill Emil for what he did to you."

"He's mine to kill." She'd never had anyone defend her honor before, or even offer her protection. The mere idea should have been ludicrous. But…it wasn't.

"He's *yours?* So you *are* in love with him? Indebted to him." Laurent backed away as if he'd been touching a beggar maid.

Cayenne bristled.

"I've never been indebted to him. And I certainly never loved him." Her words hung between them, filling the space. And then, as if it were a rubber band, the tension of the day snapped and he pounced.

They tumbled backward and landed on the bed. His strong hands ripped at her clothes, and she clawed him right back. His lips came down hard on hers, firm and punishing.

Pent up emotions surged between them, adding to the white hot lust that had consumed them both since the moment they'd met on that muggy New Orleans street. She tugged at the zipped on her boots and he left her lips long enough to pull them off. Frantic for him, she used her hands and even her feet to push his jeans down over his lean hips. Truth be told, she'd been in lust since the moment she'd laid eyes on him two weeks ago.

Longer than that really. Since he'd shown up in her dreams. Passionate dreams that left her hot, achy, needy, drenched in sweat.

Her fingers plucked at the fabric of his shirt. He peeled off her tank top, tugged off her jeans, and made short work of her lingerie. Short seconds later, they both lay naked and panting.

"Being your lover is going to become very expensive if you keep that up," she said as he tossed another shredded pair of panties over his shoulder.

He gave her a naught grin. "I can afford it."

With one hand behind her back and the other clamped over her hip, he tossed her further up on the big bed. Her heart skipped a beat as he surveyed her, head cocked to the side. His chest heaved in and out as he sucked in breath after breath and his smile lent a predatory gleam to his eyes.

She shivered with anticipation as he crawled toward her. How could he look so predatory and vulnerable at the same time? It was the same look he'd given her when he'd first woken up tied to her bed. As if he knew her so intimately, would have her at any cost and was terrified of what the attraction might cost him.

In that moment she decided there would be no more lies between them. No matter where life took her. Never again.

Even though she didn't deserve him, he deserved honesty. And right now, she had to be honest with herself too. Her body was greedy and wanton. Hot, soft, and already wet just looking at him.

He pushed her legs apart. Her fangs lengthened as she watched the strong muscles ripple under his skin, saw the strong, steady heartbeat pulsing in his neck.

"Perhaps if I drive you out of your mind with pleasure, you'll never want to leave my bed again." His smile made her breath catch. He settled between her legs, his hot breath fanning her tender flesh.

She already didn't want to leave but she couldn't tell him that. Not yet. And she wasn't far from losing her mind, of that she was sure.

"Are you wet for me, *petite*?"

She couldn't hide the evidence staring him in the face, so she bit her lip and nodded.

"I thought so. You can't deny us this."

"No," she croaked. Not when she wanted him so badly she was afraid she'd never be able to come without him.

He held her legs apart and dipped his head between her thighs. The first touch of his tongue sent her hips launching off the bed. She moaned as he licked her clit with fast little flutters that tickled her with pleasure.

He pressed his mouth against her lower lips, kissing, licking, and nibbling until she trembled on the mattress. Her insides, ready for release, quaked and coiled.

Tension rolled off of him and seeped into her. He wasn't the gentle lover she remembered. In his place was a frenzied, passionate man. The man from her dreams who made love to her as if his life depended on it. A man on a mission.

He drank from her. Devoured her. She was putty in his hands. And the look in his eyes said he knew it. Her body felt like it was made of gelatin, and it was all his doing.

She was close. So very close. A few more thrusts of that talented tongue, and she'd—

He stopped. She cried out, all pride gone, urging him to finish her off.

"Admit it," he said thickly. She lifted her head and stared down her body at him. "Admit you're mine."

"What?" He wanted to talk at a time like this?

"My mate. Admit it."

"So close..." She stabbed her heels into the comforter and pressed her hips toward him.

"Not until you admit you're mine," he demanded sharply. Sadistic.

"I admit nothing." Except that she could never go back to her former life. A life without Laurent. Without his touch. Without his voice. A life where she was nothing more than a hunter. A trained killer. A pawn on someone else's chess board. But nothing she'd done in this life made her worth loving.

Could she learn to love? Could she earn his?

Laurent watched as her head thrashed from side to side. She closed her eyes and took a shuddering breath. It was a gesture of acceptance. And reluctance. A moment of truth.

Her orgasm was only a few strokes away, and they both knew it. Right now, he'd bet, she was ready to kill for it. He let his teeth gently scrap over the little nub of flesh that would be her undoing.

He was determined to win her over. She might not believe in their love, but she couldn't deny their chemistry or how much she wanted him. Her juices flowed for him. Her nipples were hard, little rosy peaks. And her body was taunt like a violin bow. She couldn't deny what her body told her.

He slid one finger inside her slippery sheath and curled it forward. Her hips came off the bed and pressed that beautiful pink pussy into his waiting mouth. She cried out, obviously feeling the clutches of her orgasm.

"Admit it. At least to yourself. You're mine. Aren't you?" Something inside him, something dark and dangerous, needed to hear the words tumbling from her lips.

"Wolf!"

He straightened his finger and let her flesh slide from between his lips. She was going to have to learn. He wouldn't allow any other men in her life. Nor would he allow her to walk away. From this. From him. She was his. He would never lay in bed at night waiting for her. Wanting her.

Dying from the agony of losing her. Somehow he had to make her remember who she had been. What they'd had.

"What the hell are you waiting for?" she screamed, her voice bouncing off the wooden walls.

He smiled up at her. "I told you, *cheri*. I want you to admit you're my mate. *Mine.*"

"If I'm yours, then you're mine too, wolf." She reached between her legs and rubbed her clit furiously. He gave her just enough time to stoke the fire inside her before clamping a hand around her wrist and pulling her fingers away.

"Of course I'm yours, *petite*. What do you think I've been telling you?" Tired of this game, he straightened and stood at the end of the bed. Then he grabbed her ankles and pulled her toward him, flipping her over in the process.

"Laurent!"

"Enough with the games, *cheri*. You want pleasure, and so do I." He pulled her hips to the edge of the bed and covered her body with his, his front to her back. Sweat rolled down his spine as he pressed his cock against her lush, round ass.

"You seem to like using that rapier tongue as a weapon, especially where I'm concerned."

All the fight left her, and she sagged beneath him.

"I don't mean to hurt you," she said, her voice muffled by the bed. Something in her tone, about the way she submitted reminded him of the girl she'd been. She was softening.

"Then why do you?" He whispered the words against her cheek as he threaded his fingers through hers and enjoyed the feel of her curves snuggled beneath him. He'd enjoy it more once she finally submitted to him in mind *and* body.

She sighed. "I'm used to being alone, Laurent. Single. Solitary. Watching my back and protecting myself. I'm not used to wanting anything. Needing anything. *Feeling* anything."

"And I make you want, need, and feel?" If his heart could have exploded, it would have. She answered by shimmying her hips against his, her delectable, soft skin rubbing against his erection.

He slid his feet between hers and pushed her legs apart. She arched her back, and he knew it was an invitation for him to take her. She was open to him. Open and wet. He tilted his hips until the head of his shaft met the slippery entrance of her sex. Slowly, he pushed inside a fraction of an inch, gritted his teeth, and then pulled out. Over and over he teased her with just the tip and tortured himself.

"Fuck me already," she snapped, pushing back against him.

"Are you sure? Are you ready to admit that I am your mate?" There was a long pause. He wondered if she'd agree with him, just so he'd slide inside her and give them both the release they desired.

"I will try to be."

With a shout, he pressed inside her, stretching her. She moaned beneath him, and he groaned against her neck. She kept that sweet little ass high so he could slide in and out easily. And he did, over and over.

She was hot and wet, and her channel clenched him, sucking him in. He growled low in his throat. The wolf in him wanted to complete the mating ritual. Her skin was so inviting; it tempted him. Begged for his love bite.

"Harder," she cried.

Trying to ignore the call of the wolf, he turned his head, looked out the window, and thrust harder, faster. Until the bed was moving with them, creaking and scraping the old wooden floor.

"Yes!" The pleasure in her shout drove him on. He'd never had such a hard time controlling his own release. Maybe it was their position, but he decided it was Cayenne. She was his other half. Her body called to his, demanding he give her everything.

"So close. Laurent! So close. Don't—stop."

"Not…stopping."

Faster they climbed, his orgasm only a breath away. Her muscles tightened around him. Swift heat swept over his shoulders. He kept up the pace. Sank into her as deeply as he could. His jaws stretched, and his teeth sharpened against his will. His wolf was taking over. It wanted to mark her. Wanted to complete the bond.

He licked her shoulder blade, and she shivered beneath him. Unable to stop himself, he closed his teeth over the tender place between her neck and shoulder and held on as she cried out. She thrashed beneath him, and he tightened his arms around her. Moments later, her orgasm claimed her, and her pussy tightened around his cock. Her cries turned to screams of pleasure, and he groaned against her skin as his balls tightened and he let go of his control.

One final thrust into her spasming channel, and he came with a roar. His cock twitched and pulsed, spurt after spurt spilling inside her.

Finally, the throbbing subsided.

She let out an *oomph* as he collapsed on top of her, his breath ragged. His blood pounded through his veins.

I will try to be. Her words whispered through his mind. He smiled.

Drained, he pulled out and collapsed onto the bed. She pushed up further until her head was on the pillow next to him. She looked at him through those dark lashes, her eyes bright and blue.

Surprise flickered through him when she rolled toward him and kissed his lips. Soft and sweet, it was a tender kiss that said what words could not. He rolled her onto her back.

"You'll have to forgive me for my jealousy, *cheri*." Cupping her cheek in his hand he stared deep into those eyes that mesmerized him.

She hooked a hand over his bicep and placed the other over his heart. "Why would you think there was anything between me and Jules?"

Laurent huffed out a short laugh. "Have you no idea how beautiful you are?" He rained kisses across her forehead, down her nose and then slanted his lips across hers. She returned his kiss, threading her fingers through his hair.

Old uncertainties, bitter emotions warred inside him, threatening the euphoria. He battled them back and lifted his head. "I'm afraid my jealousy—it's a dreadful emotion I've dealt with for years—where you're concerned. Men used to flock to you. I'm sure they still do."

"As I'm sure women flock to you." She studied him, her eyes flicking back and forth as she took in his face.

"There's only ever been one woman for me."

Her gaze swerved to his and she stared up at him for a handful of heartbeats. With her arm still wrapped around his shoulders, she pulled herself up. Her eyelids drooped and fluttered closed just as she lifted her mouth to his.

He swept his tongue against her lips, seeking entrance. She opened immediately and wrapped her other arm around his shoulders. They moved against each other, all fury gone. In its place was a passion that took his breath away.

"I can't believe you're still hard," she whispered when he left her mouth to trail kisses down her throat. Their movements against each other were slow and searching. It was a dance...a slow dance.

"I could make love to you all night, *cheri*," his whispered and then proceeded to keep his word.

9

Standing in the kitchen just before sunset the next day, Cayenne wondered if she'd ever get used to being awake during the day. Even in the safety of the home it still felt unnatural. Unlike Laurent, she'd slept most of the day away.

Her gaze wandered over the large, homey space. Like everything else about the Deveraux plantation, no expense was spared it seemed. She had little use for such a room. But Laurent was in a discussion with his brother and had suggested that Amanda could use some help.

Angelica came through the side door, cargo shorts slung low on her hips and raindrops dotting her pink t-shirt. She smiled at Cayenne and dropped a basket full of leaves on the center island.

"Herbs," she said as if that explained everything.

Cayenne felt uncomfortable. She hadn't fed for two days. It had taken all her willpower not to drink from Laurent during this morning's love making session. Over the years she'd learned to control her urges. To subsist on little blood. But she'd have to drink soon.

Amanda backed out of the walk-in pantry, humming a tune Cayenne didn't recognize. She stayed frozen just inside the doorway, unsure what to do or say. She wasn't good with people. She killed people. Her promise to try to be his mate was coming back to haunt her in the bright of the day. Laurent was crazy if he expected her to fit in here.

"Hi there," Amanda said in her sweet southern accent. She deposited an armful of groceries onto the island and leaned down to inhale the fragrance of the herbs. "Come on Cayenne, we won't bite."

The little southern belle waved Cayenne over.

"I'm not sure what I'm doing here," Cayenne said and took a step closer. They might not bite. But she did. Not that she would ever bite them. That wouldn't be good manners.

"Hiding out from a bad ex, it sounds like," Angel said. Cayenne studied the other woman. Warm blond hair. Big expressive yes. A sparkling smile. She very much fit her name.

"I don't know why Laurent insists we lay low," she said before she could stop herself. It wasn't like her to open up. Certainly not to strangers. But as Amanda smiled up at Angel, Cayenne realized it was hard to stay tight lipped around a woman like her. She seemed so natural and friendly. Feminine and unafraid. Everything the women Cayenne knew were not.

"It's for your protection I imagine," the southern belle said as she started filling a large copper pot with water.

Cayenne stepped farther into the room and tried not to let her annoyance show. "I don't need protection. Didn't Laurent tell you what I do for a living?"

"You assassinate bad people," Angel supplied.

Cayenne inclined her head in agreement.

"Is it so wrong that he wants to protect you, Cayenne? He is your mate after all." Amanda glanced at Angel and Cayenne once again saw the longing in their eyes. Though they both shared an unbreakable bond with their men, they didn't have the predestined mark to prove it. They were not immortal. They would grow old and pass on. And Sebastian and Jules would lose them forever.

Cayenne dropped her gaze to the brick floor and felt an odd stirring in the region of her heart. How sad for them. How awful to know that truth. And even worse, here she was in their kitchen, reminding them of the very thing they could never have and yet, so obviously wanted.

"I suppose not," she said carefully. She knew

that she didn't need Laurent's protection. Laurent probably knew it too. She gathered that he was buying time. Hoping to integrate her with his pack. Waiting for her to remember what they shared. For her to fall in love with him again.

And that was the problem. She may never remember what they shared. But her body remembered. Her heart remembered. And every night when he filled her dreams she was a little more sure that what he told her was the truth. But even if everything was true, was she capable of love? Was she capable, after all this time and all her training, of opening herself to someone else?

She watched as the other two women moved harmoniously around the kitchen. It was like a dance they'd performed a hundred times. Chopping vegetables, measuring ingredients, boiling pasta. The scene was terribly cozy.

"Have a seat," Amanda said and nodded to the four tall bar chairs lined up along one side of the island.

Cayenne took a deep breath and sat down. She kept her fingers laced and rested them against the cool, smooth stone surface and tried not to pay attention to the sound of their blood pulsing through their veins. *Act normal.* She could do that, right? Just for a few hours. Just long enough to fit in like Laurent wanted.

"Do you prefer to be called Cayenne or Violet?" Amanda asked from across the island.

Cayenne hadn't really thought about it. She'd never been particularly fond of her name. But then she'd never had any reason to change it. But whenever Laurent called her Violet...something inside her fluttered. A memory?

"Cayenne is fine," she decided. Better to keep things as they were. No use rushing to change everything at once.

Despite her feelings for Laurent, she couldn't stay here. With his pack. Could she?

Would that be crazy? Looking around the high end kitchen with its recessed lighting and fancy cabinets made her feel out of place.

She thought of the way Jules had reacted yesterday. Could she become a woman deserving of Laurent?

"You'll have to forgive us, Cayenne," Amanda said and then glanced over at Angel. "We've never had a vampire join us for dinner before. In fact, we're still getting used to the whole fur and paws routine."

"It's fine. I don't eat human food." Not any more. But sometimes she craved a croissant more than her next drink.

Angel sidled up to Amanda, a nervous expression on her face. "What, ugh, do you eat then? If you don't mind me asking."

Cayenne's eyebrows arched up at the young woman's bravado and her lips twitched. Angel gave an anxious laugh. Cayenne, for the first time she could remember, laughed. The movement shook her shoulders and she felt a jolt of pure joy.

A bemused smile curved her lips. Nothing, not even sex with Laurent had made her feel that good. It was like being unleashed, unlocked from her prison.

Angel and Amanda looked startled, but then they joined in the laughter.

"Mostly these days I drink from bagged sources. Not unlike your canned goods." A marvelous invention, that.

Amanda nodded, taking the information in stride. Angel looked a little less uneasy.

"You're not on the menu, if that's what you're asking," Cayenne said and gave the woman what she hoped was a friendly smile.

Their eyes went wide. "Wow. Do those hurt?"

Cayenne flicked her tongue over her fangs. "No."

Laurent paused outside the kitchen doorway, astonished to hear his mate's laughter. The sweet sound hit him straight in the heart like a dagger. He remembered it all too well. Had missed it so much. To hear it again felt like a dream. And yet jealousy gnawed at him. *He* hadn't made her laugh.

He pushed the evil emotion away and listened to the womens' quiet voices.

She was fitting in faster than he'd thought she would. Especially considering he wasn't sure she wanted to fit in. She'd promised to try to be his mate. And he knew that he needed to win Amanda's vote if he and Cayenne were to continue living here. But just how permenant Cayenne wanted their current living situation to be…he wasn't sure.

Frustrated by the uncertainty that had eaten at him for the past two days he turned and strode back down the wide hall and reentered Sebastian's office. Jules stood at the window looking out at the manicured grounds, ever on alert. Sebastian sat behind his desk, studying a document.

If Laurent and more importantly, Cayenne, could win Amanda's vote, he knew it wouldn't be long before Sebastian could be persuaded.

"They're laughing," Laurent said, bemused. He took a seat in the wide leather sofa across from the floor to ceiling windows and dragged a hand down his face.

"Laughing?" Jules asked.

"I haven't heard her laugh in over two hundred years," Laurent mused, gazing at the wildly patterned Persian rug. *Two hundred years.*

"What could they have to laugh about?" Sebastian asked. He shifted in his seat, obviously still uneasy with Violet's presence. Laurent wasn't sure if he was still worried about Laurent's broken heart or the possibility that Cayenne might try to kill him again. Or more importantly if she posed a risk to the rest of the Pack.

But Laurent trusted her.

No matter what she called herself, to him, she'd always be Violet. To his brother and cousin's she would always be the woman who broke his heart.

The three of them glanced at each other. Laurent shrugged. Jules frowned. Sebastian pursed his lips and went back to reading.

CAYENNE HAD NEVER HAD friends before, at least none that she remembered. The people in her life were acquaintances at best. Mentors. Fellow students. Targets. But never friends.

Which is why when Amanda reached for Cayenne's wrist, pulled her down from her bar chair, and then proceeded to teach her how to make old fashioned biscuits, Cayenne was completely surprised. And humbled.

She'd never done anything so domestic. Listening to Amanda's instructions, watching her demonstration, Cayenne could see that cooking was much like learning how to use a sword. Baking was pretty exacting. Proper ingredients in the right measurements, and lots of practice, Amanda had said, were the key to fabulous biscuits.

The dough squished beneath her fingers.

"You're doing good," Amanda said, her voice full of encouragement.

Why were they being so nice?

"You want to pat the dough flat. About an inch thick," Amanda directed and then placed a round, silver biscuit cutter onto the edge of the large cutting board.

Cayenne did as she was told, using her palms to press the dough as evenly as possible. "It's springy," she murmured, more to herself than her teacher.

"Hmm huh. This is great grandma's recipe. A favorite among the Deveraux men."

Cayenne glanced at the southern belle standing at her side. What was it like to be so accepted? To have a place you belonged?

Ignoring the thoughts and the longing that went along with them, she continued flattening the dough.

"You're pretty good at that," Angel said from her station at the stove. "Are you sure you've never done that before?"

Cayenne looked at the disc of dough. A memory sliced through her, sharp and fast. Smaller hands. An old, well worn table. And the sound of laughter. She shook it off. "I'm not sure of anything anymore."

"Now, the fun part," Amanda chimed in. "Dip the cutter in flour." She dropped a handful of white powder next to the cutter. "And then start cutting. Just press down evenly, rock it side to side a bit, twist and lift."

Cayenne reached for the round silver utensil. Wrapping her fingers around the handle she aimed it at the dough as Amanda had instructed. She pressed down. The cutting board groaned under her strength. Oops.

She jerked her hand back and a biscuit hurtled through the air. Flour exploded through the kitchen. Amanda and Angel gasped. Cayenne twisted her body in a lightning fast move and caught the biscuit in her hand. Milky white powder showered down around them.

The kitchen went completely silent. She met their gaze.

"Holy cow. That was impressive," Angel exclaimed. "I wish I'd gotten that on camera. But then, I'm not even sure what shutter speed to set to catch something moving that fast." She laughed, easing the tension.

Amanda glanced down at the biscuit in Cayenne's hand. Cayenne waited for a reprimand.

"Your first biscuit. Good job." She plucked it from Cayenne's hand and deposited it on a baking sheet. "Maybe a little less force next time," she said with a smile.

"Whoa, who set off the flour bomb?" She turned to see Jules entering the kitchen, his long legs ate up the space to Angel and he kissed her neck.

"That would be me," Cayenne admitted.

"Are those great gram's biscuits?" the werewolf asked, his gaze zeroing in on the slab of dough. His stomach growled.

Cayenne couldn't help but join in the laughter. How had she missed this? Her whole life seemed so cold, so sterile. And this homey kitchen was the exact opposite. Well loved. Lived in. Appreciated.

She shifted from one foot to the other and glanced at the gouge she'd left in the cutting board. Another sign she didn't belong here.

"I think I've done enough damage for one day," Cayenne said, setting the biscuit cutter carefully on the counter.

"You don't have to go," Amanda said.

"Thanks for teaching me."

"Join us for dinner tonight," Angel called as Cayenne hurried from the room and took the stairs two at a time. In her room she settled into the well loved wingback chair in front of the window and looked out. She sucked in one deep breath after another. *Hyperventilate much?* she thought wryly.

The sun was setting, bathing the forest in warm honey colored light. She drug both hands down her face. Emotions she'd managed to hold at bay for centuries bombarded her. She couldn't put her finger on the exact moment the change had occurred, all she knew was that she wasn't the same woman who'd arrived in New Orleans two weeks ago.

"Why are you hiding in here?" Laurent's deep, sexy voice cut through her trip down memory lane.

She jerked her head left and took in the handsome man who filled the doorway. Could the fates really have picked someone so...masculine, so big to be her mate?

Watching his long legs move beneath the tight denim did funny things to her insides. He squatted in front of her and draped an arm over her legs.

"Now, tell me...why are you hiding?"

"I'm not hiding. I went to the kitchen like you asked." She let her hands drop to her thighs and noticed a trace of flour at her wrist.

"How'd it go?" His words sounded casual, but she felt a deeper concern behind them.

"I made biscuits." She wiped the flour away.

He reached up and used his thumb to wipe a smudge from her cheek. "I can see that," he said softly. His gorgeous brown eyes locked with hers and she wondered if this is how it had happened all those years ago. How she'd fallen in love with him. Had he used that soft, sure tone? Had he stared into her eyes until she couldn't breath and her clothing felt too tight?

"Evidently I'm stronger than I thought. There

was a mishap with the cutting board and then the whole flying biscuit fiasco followed by a flour shower," she said in a rush.

His eyes sparkled as he laughed. "I would have paid good money to see that."

"As opposed to bad money?"

"Why are you up here by yourself, *cheri*?"

Why did he have to speak to her like that? So softly? So sweetly? And use endearments, good heavens it made her melt. And she couldn't afford to melt. Not now. She had to stay strong. Resolute. She had to think. And it was damn near impossible to think with the sexy hunk of werewolf kneeling in front of her, touching her so gently, speaking to her so sweetly.

"Surely Amanda didn't kick you out of the kitchen."

Cayenne shook her head.

"I just need some time to myself. To think." Now if she could just keep telling herself that. And actually follow through.

"You do too much of that. Sometimes you need to let yourself feel."

Cayenne knew it was safest to change the subject lest she be drawn into an exchange about…feelings. Something she didn't want to address. "Do you really think it's necessary to hide out here? We're endangering your family unnecessarily."

She didn't want to be responsible if something

happened to his brother. Or cousins. Or heaven forbid Amanda and Angelica.

"This is the best place to be. A full on battle between us and them in the middle of the city wouldn't be good. Even in a town like New Orleans that'd be attention we don't need."

After a few moments, she nodded. He was right. She glanced out the window and sighed.

Just like that, the spell was over. Laurent pushed to his feet and stepped to the window, remembering her innocence all those years ago. When she'd never worried about things like vampire attacks. Those wide, trustful eyes had she looked at him as if no one else on the planet existed.

Emil had changed all of that. Stolen her from him. And she was right. There was a potential for danger if they weren't prepared for Emil's attack.

When Laurent got his hands on the bastard he would make him pay for ever harming Violet and her family.

10

Werewolves had a voracious appetite. She'd known that, but she'd never actually watched them eat. Settled between Amanda and Laurent at the large round dining table, she had a front row seat for the activities.

"Here's the one Cayenne made," Amanda said, setting the golden biscuit on Laurent's plate.

He murmured his thanks.

She knew that he was still mulling over her words. And though she knew his family came from a long line of warriors, hunters, something still didn't feel right about hiding out here. Putting others at risk for something she herself should have ended more than a century ago.

Her guilt ate at her. So did her hunger.

Jules cracked a joke and everyone else laughed, but she kept her focus on the empty plate in front of her.

Amanda leaned over. "I know you don't eat human food," she whispered, "but I felt weird not having a plate in front of you. Call it southern hospitality."

"It's fine."

Cayenne hated the tension in the air. Normally the thick anticipation powered her. But not right now. Amanda and Angel had made her feel welcome. But the looks that Jules and Sebastian shot her way were filled with skepticism. And watching them all laugh together, eat together, the cozy scene made her feel like an outsider with her nose pressed against the glass. Worse than that, she felt like a fraud.

Trying to fit in when she had no business being here. No business putting their lives in danger.

"I'm sorry if I'm being rude," she whispered to Amanda.

"Don't worry about it. Think of all the calories you're saving yourself from." She gave that impish grin of hers.

"What are you two whispering about?" Sebastian asked quietly, his arm stretched along the back of Amanda's chair.

Cayenne glanced past the woman between them and saw him pop an entire biscuit in his mouth.

"I'm trying to make our guest comfortable,"

Amanda replied and pegged her husband with a play-nice look.

Cayenne tried not to notice the vein pulsing at Amanda's neck. The safest place to look was at the table. At the mountain of beef, chicken, bread and the occasional vegetable.

"Yeah, it's not every day we have a bloodsucker at the table," Jules muttered.

"Jules Deveraux," Angelica exclaimed, her whole body shifting in her chair as she pegged her fiancé with a fiery look. He immediately looked sheepish.

"He states the obvious, Angel," Cayenne said.

"It doesn't give him an excuse to lose what manners his mother gave him. You apologize, wolf or I'll whallop you," Amanda demanded.

Jules glanced at Sebastian, then regarded Amanda before his gaze fell on Cayenne. "Sorry, Cayenne."

The meal progressed as if Jules hadn't spoken and the tension seemed to ease a bit. Food kept the men occupied and Angel and Amanda kept up a fluid stream of chatter, drawing occasional comments from the others.

Cayenne watched as Burke finished off his fourth steak. Unbelievable.

Amanda must have noticed her watching the feast. "I know…they eat a lot. It took me a while to get used to it."

"I'm a growin' boy," Jules teased and patted

his flat stomach. Her lips curved upward. He seemed like the youngest of the group. Always getting into trouble, speaking before he thought, cracking jokes. Charm. That's what saved him.

"Are you feeling all right?" Amanda asked.

"You look a little pale…" Angel chimed in.

Cayenne heard the words, waited for Jules to crack a joke, and fought to stay in a serene place. A place where hunger did not exist. Where she wasn't thirsty. A place where she didn't crave blood.

It was a place she'd gone to many times over the years as she waited for a target or did extensive surveillance.

She'd honed the skill. Perfected it. But normally, she was so focused on her mission and there were no distractions to pull her from her concentration.

A loud, hungry pack of werewolves was definitely a distraction. As was the sound of their combined heartbeats.

If she could just forget them. Go away. Far away. Drink…

"Maybe she just needs to nibble on Laurent a bit," Burke said and laughter cut through her focus.

As if the thought had occurred to him for the first time, Laurent swiveled around in his seat. "*Are* you hungry?"

Her focus shattered at the intensity of his words. "A little bit," she whispered.

He pushed away from the table. "Excuse us," he told the others and pulled her chair back.

Not wanting to make a scene, she stood. He reached for her hand, held it for a moment as he stared down at her. Emotions flickered through his eyes.

She was thankful for the reprieve as it was far easier to control the hunger when she was isolated. When she couldn't hear a pulse.

"Thank you," she murmured as he led her from the room.

"You should have told me." His words were quiet but anger rippled off of him.

Her feet hit the top of the landing and she turned to him with raised eyebrows. "What?" Her voice was shrill and she hoped the others hadn't heard her.

"You should have told me you needed to feed."

Her temper snapped and she put her hands on her hips. "Of course I need to feed. I'm a vampire not a ghost."

He started to reach for her but she backed away. "I just meant…I don't know your schedule."

"Do you want me to draw you up a spreadsheet?" She turned and marched toward their room.

"Cayenne," he called after her. "This is new for me, *cheri*."

She heard his footsteps on the old wooden floor behind her but she didn't slow down. Annoyed at the whole situation, she ran her tongue over her fangs.

Large, warm hands clamped around her upper arms and he gently turned her so that she was facing him. As quickly as it'd come, the anger died and in its place, passion and remorse. She realized then that he'd been angry with himself. Upset that he hadn't seen to her needs.

He cupped her cheek and stared down at her for long silent moments.

She felt her resolve dissolving. He reached for the top button of his shirt and slipped it through the hole. Then the next and the next. His slow, steady work revealed the broad, muscled chest she'd come to memorize. She was helpless to do anything but stare at the perfection before her.

Against her better judgment, she slid her palms up the smooth plain of his stomach and over his pecs. He sucked in a breath and covered her hands with his. She closed her eyes, relishing the warmth that soaked into her skin.

"Drink." The word was simple. As much a demand as desperation. And undeniably erotic.

The vein at his neck pulsed, calling to her. Begging for her fangs. Her breathing shallowed and lust zinged through her bloodstream.

What would he taste like?

She'd never taken blood from a werewolf before. Nor anyone who knew her past. Could his blood contain memories of her, of her past self? Could she deny herself that? Could she fight the hunger?

He tipped his head to the side, offering himself to her. The simple gesture echoed through her. He really was a nice guy. A descent guy. A guy she could have loved…

And with that simple gesture, the acceptance and hope written on his face, she lost her fight.

Leaning forward, she kissed her way up his chest and then eased up onto her tip-toes. Snaking an arm around his broad shoulders, she licked a trail up to his neck. His pulse jumped beneath her tongue. She moaned. He smelled so good. Masculine, earthy, sexy.

They shared a breath as anticipation rippled through her. *Taste.* Her fangs grazed his skin and a sigh whispered through his lips. His hands settled on her hips, holding her close, encouraging her.

All of the seconds that they'd been together had been leading up to this moment. She was sure of it. Living and dying, past and present were meeting in this singular point in time. And somehow she knew that after she'd taken his blood, absorbed his memories, her life would never be the same again.

Cayenne sank her fangs into his flesh and his blood ran over her tongue.

Ecstasy.

She closed her eyes and moaned against him.

Delicious. His fingers flexed into her skin. White hot lust rushed through her, tightening her breasts, setting her skin on fire, making her most feminine places contract with desire.

And then, all at once, his memories assailed her. Memories of her as a girl, ripe in the threshold of womanhood. Her hair, her eyes, so familiar. So similar to her own. And yet, so different. Her hair had a curl to it, it bounced as she moved. Her eyes were young and hopeful, not jaded with the ways of the world. Not knowledgeable in the ways of men.

And her smile. Wide. Genuinely happy.

She hadn't felt that sort of happiness…ever.

One by one, Laurent's past days filled her mind. Filled her heart. He really had loved her. Completely. Hopelessly. He'd been ridiculed for his love.

Pain consumed her. His pain. Pain from the wounds inflicted by others. Pain from her disappearance. The pain of being alone without the one he loved.

Too much. It was too much.

He couldn't still love her, not like that. Not so…

She removed her fangs and licked away the remaining drops of blood.

"I do, you know," he whispered, finally breaking through her mental barrier. It should have surprised her. She'd worked hard to protect herself. But being in his arms, tasting him, her guard was down.

Worse than that, the protective shell she'd insulated herself with was completely shattered.

11

Cayenne thumbed the blade of her sword, testing the sharpness. Not sharp enough. She wiped the blade with a cloth, enjoying the way the gleaming silver caught the light.

Night had fallen over the lovely estate, shrouding it in inky darkness. The large armory provided her with solace and quiet in the middle of the night. The wolves had done well with the old parlor, turning it into a treasure of weapons and fitness equipment while still respecting the architecture.

She liked that they hadn't left the interior of their home with the stuffy relics from ages past. Without ornate furnishings covered in knick-knacks she could enjoy the house in her original Greek Revival beauty.

It wasn't her shift to be on watch, but she hadn't been able to sleep either. She'd left

Laurent's bed to prepare for the battle she felt coming. It was only a matter of time.

Cayenne ran the sharpening stone over the blade, careful to keep the angle just so. Over and over, she repeated the action, honing the edge then switching to a higher grit stone. It was a movement she could do in her sleep, drilled into her many years ago by the Madame.

The Madame's eerie black eyes and alabaster skin were fresh in Cayenne's mind. Ironic that she could remember the devil who'd trained her to kill but she could not remember her past self. Her family. The man she'd loved.

She was certain of it now. Laurent wasn't lying to save his skin. He wasn't a fabulous actor with an incredible story. He spoke the truth. His memories of her were real. And potent. No wonder he'd been heartbroken, they'd been very much in love. Even against the odds.

There was so much evidence against Emil. More than the feeling she'd always felt in her gut. To his displeasure she'd been immune from him since the start. At least, what she remembered as the start. Even as he'd fed her the story of how he'd saved her from death, given her a new life, she hadn't felt indebted to him. Never that.

She'd felt his greed. The poison inside him. The lust seeping from his pores. Even after all this time he followed her around the globe, showing up unexpectedly. And now that she'd been reunited with Laurent… she cupped the sand paper in her hand and slid it down the blade. Emil would be out for blood. It was only a matter of time before he tracked her.

He must have felt the change in her. The pleasure she'd felt when Laurent touched her. She hadn't been the same since he'd woken up chained to her bed, calling her Violet.

She gazed out at the ancient Oak trees bathed in moonlight. Deep down she'd known this day was coming, almost from that first moment she'd woken in Emil's arms. The only way to get away from him, truly away from him, was end it, end *him*, once and for all, with her own blade.

Someone knocked on the door and she swiveled to see André standing in the doorway. "Am I interrupting?"

She shook her head.

He strode into the room, his movements graceful and so similar to Laurent's. What had this family done to win the gene-pool-lottery? All of them, incredibly handsome, oozing masculinity and graceful too. Wasn't there a law against that?

"Laurent says you studied in Asia," he said, nodding toward the blade in her hands.

"Mongolia. With Madame." Where Cayenne had once felt pride at that, of who'd trained her, now she felt little more than irritation at her naivety. She'd been so distraught after Jean-Claude's death, so shattered from the werewolf attack that almost left her dead, Madame's school had seemed the perfect solution. Learn how to fight. How to kill. How to defend herself. If only she'd been more properly trained, Jean-Claude might not be dead.

But she'd stopped mourning his loss ages ago.

"Ya know you can leave at any time." His voice was level, unjudgemental. The only Deveraux other than Laurent to not look at her with censure in his eyes. He stepped to a glass walled cabinet and opened the doors.

"I know."

He pulled out a sword, not that different from her own. "I got this in battle. Little Japanese man. He never had a chance." There was sorrow in his eyes and regret in his voice. "A sword is no match for a bullet," he added grimly.

"Depends on who's holding the sword," she said.

He smiled and she wondered how in the world he was not mated. Had she not been…with… Laurent she could have easily fallen under André's spell.

"Well said my vampire friend." He removed the sheath from his sword and studied the blade.

She cocked her head to the side and watched him. "Friend?" she asked cautiously.

His gaze met hers. She felt the intensity of his deep brown eyes all the way to her core. "You are not my enemy, are you?"

Perhaps she had been a week ago. "No. I'm not your enemy."

He nodded once. It was as if his mind were made up and he was pleased with the outcome. Somehow she felt outmaneuvered; it was a very rare and uncomfortable feeling. One she tried to avoid at all costs.

"So why do you stay?" he asked, tightening his grip on the hilt.

"Laurent is a good man."

"I agree."

"He doesn't deserve to die."

"No, he doesn't." He made a few practice swings. "Whattya, say Cayenne. Want to see if this old wolf still knows his way around a sword?"

She chuckled softly and stood. "I'll go easy on you."

As she settled into her en-guarde stance and lifted her sword above her head, an eerie calm passed through her. It was a ballsy move, holding her sword up when she should have held it down to protect herself. Adrenaline surged through her system making her feel alive. Her muscles tightened, ready for battle.

André took a step toward her. Her reflexes didn't fail her. She parried left, blocking his blade.

She kept her movements slow to match his, ensuring each of her movements was precise and correctly executed. He stepped to the right and again, she mirrored the step, watching him closely, detecting any weakness.

He advanced again with a thrust. She parried left again. He retreated, then slashed. Metal clanged against metal.

"So why," he began, parrying left, then right. "Do you think Laurent is in danger?"

"Emil," she said, blocking his movement. "He most likely saw us escape together."

André lunged, his blade coming down hard. Cayenne stepped right, using all her strength to fend off the attack. Her blade hovered, parallel to the floor. Then with the speed of her kind, she whirled right, tucking her sword as she spun to the far side of the room.

"Nice move."

"They'll move fast too. The others. If they follow us."

"You don't sound so sure."

"Emil is a wild card."

André waved her forward. This time, Cayenne attacked. He blocked her skillfully. Quickly. But not quickly enough. Vampires were fast. And strong.

Werewolves were all brute force. She was agile, nimbly stepping right, delivering a blow with the flat of her blade across his back. He staggered forward.

Balance regained, he turned toward her.

"Sometimes I've gone a whole decade without

seeing or hearing from him. He shows up randomly. Uninvited."

He lunged again. Paried left. Right. Swept his blade through the air to cut her off at the knees. She leapt upwards, landing on a long credenza. He raised his sword. She cart-wheeled through the air, landing behind him. Holding the tip of her blade to the center of his back, she sucked in a breath.

"Emil may not show himself for weeks. Months. Or he may come tonight. I do my best to block him out."

"Does that go for Laurent too?"

"I didn't know about him."

"Now that you do?" he asked over his shoulder.

"Laurent isn't my concern right now. Emil is. The only way I'll ever be free of him, of this life, is if I take his."

André faked left, stabbing his blade into the wooden floor while spinning right. He caught her around the middle. They hit the floor with a thud. Her sword skittered away and her breath whooshed from her lungs as her skull connected with the floor.

"Good move," she whispered. Damn that hurt.

"Why don't you go after him?"

"Laurent's right. Home court advantage is best."

"For Laurent maybe."

"I'm learning my way around."

He shoved away from her, clasping her right hand as he went and pulled her to her feet. Without pausing he spun right and retrieved his sword.

Never let go of your sword. Madame's words echoed through her mind. *Never let down your guard.*

Cayenne performed a back-handspring to recover her weapon. André charged her. Their swords came together with a clang. Tiny fragments of metal sheared off like sparks.

She held the hilt with one hand, the back of the blade with the other, holding off his sword, resisting his strength. He leaned closer, using his body weight.

"You love him."

"I—I believe I did. Once upon a time…"

"I think you still do. Why else would you be here? When surely a woman of your talent could track and dispatch Emil by yourself?"

With that, he backed away, his gaze locked with hers. She stood there, speechless. In love with Laurent? The idea was—She'd known him for five days.

Okay, two hundred years or so, if she were being technical.

André sheathed his sword and put it back in the display case.

She felt steamrolled. Set-up. He'd been testing

her. Not just her skills as a fighter, but her feelings toward his cousin. Deep down, she had to admire that about him. Killing two birds with one well aimed stone.

Just before he exited the room he stopped and glanced at her. "It's nice to have a woman in the house who knows her way around a sword."

The moment after he stepped from the room, Laurent strode in. She sheathed her sword, ready for a break. She'd finish sharpening her weapon tomorrow.

"Don't even think about it," he said, pacing back and forth in front of her, his large hands hooked over lean hips.

"Think about what?"

"Tracking Emil on your own. We agreed this is the best place for us to be."

"Who said anything about tracking Emil?" So he'd been listening to their discussion. She was finding her mate to be rather jealous. Not that she could blame him really. With all the time lost…

He let out a frustrated sigh and looked skyward as if trying to regain his patience. She deposited her sword on the credenza and turned to face him.

"André said that. And I won't say it hasn't crossed my mind. But you're right in that a brawl with the vamps would be better in the middle of nowhere than the center of a city, even one as haunted as New Orleans."

That seemed to sooth him somewhat.

She closed the distance between him and ran her hands up his chest, relishing the warmth he radiated. "You must learn to trust, Laurent."

"I don't trust much of anything." His response was swift, premeditated.

"Not even me?" she asked.

He stared down into the beautiful blue eyes he'd known for so long. Trust her. Did he trust her? She was everything to him. Always had been. But she was right. He did have a problem with trust. He trusted Burke. And his cousins. But somewhere along the way, he'd lost faith in people.

And deep down, he wasn't entirely sure he trusted her not to leave him again.

Though, she was a different woman than the one who'd tried to kill him a week ago she was also different from the young woman he'd fallen in love with so long ago. Could he trust her with his heart again?

She smiled up at him and he felt the punch to his gut her smiles always brought. So lovely. So kissable. Her eyes alight with mischief.

She turned and sauntered away, her hips swinging in a sexy strut. Why did he get the feeling she knew something he didn't?

12

Cayenne tried to focus on the page but she'd been sitting in this chair for over an hour and hadn't read a single word. The living room was silent with nothing to distract her. Except for her thoughts, which constantly strayed to the conversation she'd had with André two nights ago. He could either see into the future or was full of it.

The sound of a chair scraping across wood drew her attention to the dining room. Burke settled himself into a chair and tore off a hunk of bread. Everyone else had finished eating and headed off to other parts of the house. Laurent had murmured something about a meeting with Sebastian about the company. She'd chosen to stay out of the way and get some reading in. Books were a favorite past time between missions.

Since she'd arrived Burke had walked the property line every morning and every night. It annoyed her that Laurent had forbidden her from leaving the house. She wasn't an infant that needed protecting. She flicked her hair over her shoulder and tucked her feet beneath her.

And at the same time she understood why he was so protective. He didn't want anything to happen to her. He didn't want anything to separate them again. He hadn't asked to hear the words. Hell, he hadn't even said them. But she could see the love in his eyes every time he looked at her. Something inside her fluttered.

How could André possibly know how she felt about Laurent when she wasn't even sure how she felt herself? Other than the fact her blood boiled ever time he was near and she felt all tingly whenever she thought of him. Sleeping in his arms was the most relaxing thing she'd ever done. It was as if for the briefest of moments she could truly let her guard down and just be herself. Not a warrior. Not an assassin.

A woman.

No games. No lies. No hidden agenda. She could just be. She could relax. She could feel safe.

She met Burke's glance across the dinner table. Was he lonely? Truth be told, the big man intimidated her a little bit. He was far bigger than his brother and cousins. And Madame had always warned her to watch out for the silent ones. There was a hidden depth there, she'd said.

She was sure of all the men in the house that,

as Laurent's brother, he would have questions for her. But he remained silent as he ate.

She flicked her gaze back to the book. What if André was wrong? Being in love and admitting to being mates were two very different things. What if she could never love Laurent as she had before?

She knew the answer to that question.

We've all got questions, vamp. Like how long will you be around for this time? Burke's words rumbled through her mind. She felt the intensity of his gaze, his concern for his brother, all the way to her bones. *Just don't get his hopes up if yer gonna be leavin' him again.*

She didn't know what to tell him. She wasn't sure of much. Not her past and certainly not her future.

He stuck another chunk of bread in his mouth and then carried his empty plate into the kitchen.

Why did everyone think it was her fault for leaving Laurent in the first place? As if she had any control over that. Maybe she had. She couldn't know. But she didn't think she would have gone willingly. Did they all know something she didn't? Had she really broken Laurent's heart on purpose?

Her gaze fell on the chess board on the table next to her. Jean Claude had taught her how to play. Those lessons seemed like an eternity ago. In fact, she could barely remember his face now.

But she could still remember the ancient chess

board where she'd learned to play. Funny how life had turned out to be very similar to a game of chess. A series of movements, forward, back, side to side. And all for what? To capture someone else's king?

So much battle and warfare.

Over and over she'd made her moves. Being a good soldier. Followed orders. Slain the king.

She was nothing more than a pawn.

She gulped. She'd lost her life in the process. And why? To get away from Emil? To protect herself? She'd protected herself too well. She couldn't even remember the love of her life. A love so strong that Laurent had mourned her for centuries.

A single tear rolled down her cheek. She'd lost so much. Experienced so much. And yet, when it came down to what mattered. What really mattered…Regardless of all the missions she'd completed for Madame, she'd never felt complete. Whole.

She brushed away the tear as the white pieces blurred together with the black.

Being with Laurent…she felt complete. Whole. Loved. Accepted. Like she had a future that mattered. Like she could control her destiny. She let out a shaky laugh as happiness bubbled inside her.

Funny how she'd lived for so long and never known. Never understood herself. What she really wanted. What she dreamed of. What she needed.

A heartbeat drew her attention away from the board and she looked over her shoulder to find Jules leaning against the doorframe.

He looked at her for a long moment before glancing at the board in front of her. Then he chewed his lip as if making a decision. Mind made up, he stepped across the cozy room and took the seat opposite her.

She watched every movement, waiting for him to say something. Another biting comment perhaps.

Wordlessly he moved a white pawn two spaces. She raised her eyebrows. Then made a move of her own. He countered.

She studied the board and moved a knight.

He glanced out at the night. "I apologize for what I said the other night."

"There's no need to apologize."

He moved another piece. "You're leaving then?"

It was her turn to study the board. "No."

She couldn't leave Laurent. Didn't want to.

She moved her rook into position, deftly swiping his piece in the process.

"No?"

"I'm still waiting on Emil to make his move." She set his piece to the left of the board, a trace of satisfaction curving her lips.

"What if he doesn't make a move?"

She glanced up into his deep brown eyes. "Then I guess you're just stuck with me."

He laughed. Actually tipped back his head and laughed. The sound was rich and happy and made her feel like less of an outsider. "I can imagine many things worse than having you in the Pack."

They made another volley of moves. "Emil will come. Now that I'm with Laurent again he'll feel threatened. The bastard has always wanted me for himself. It's probably why he changed me in the first place."

"You're with Laurent now?" He eyed her skeptically, as if looking for a sign of her change of heart. She doubted he'd see the change in her.

She was tired of running. Tired of traveling the world to complete another job. She was tired of the death. All of the sorrow that filled her nights. She was tired of the evil that surrounded her.

Laurent was like a ray of bright light. A stream of warmth she yearned to step into.

"I'm his mate," she said simply.

"You think Emil knows that?"

"Emil smelled Laurent all over me. I think he knew how much Laurent meant to me and that by being with him again..."

"Your memory could return."

She nodded and captured another of his pieces.

"But who knows what Emil is thinking. I prefer not to try. He's mounted a small army. I doubt he'd just give me up without a fight."

"Give you up?"

"He's my sire. Nothing more."

"But he wanted more."

"Since the very beginning."

"You're a strong woman."

"I'm a smart woman. You don't need to be strong to turn down a slug like Emil."

"I imagine you'd need to be very strong. Vampires are known for the mind-altering powers."

"I guess I just have a good resistance to bull shit then."

He laughed. "Check."

Cayenne lowered her gaze to the checkered board, a familiar hum of adrenaline flowing through her veins. Time to go in for the kill.

A slow smile curved her lips as her hand hovered above the board. She moved her knight into position, taking his queen.

"Checkmate."

13

Laurent slipped from the bed and stepped to the window. Cayenne raked her gaze over his broad shoulders, down over that gloriously naked and perfectly round ass. She'd memorized the feel of his hard body gliding against hers during the past seven days.

Enjoying anything as much as she enjoyed sex with Laurent bordered on obsession. But try as she might—and she'd tried hard these past few days—she couldn't deny her need to feel him inside her. And he certainly didn't object.

In fact, he'd given her *the look* so often she was starting to feel sunburned. Not a good thing for a vamp.

"André says the hurricane'll be here in the next two or three days," he said. Thunder rumbled, disturbing an otherwise peaceful evening.

"I'm not used to all this stormy weather," she said, getting out of bed. She crossed the room and hugged him from behind.

He chuckled. Her fingers glided across his abs, and she relished the warmth of his skin. How had he come to mean so much to her so quickly?

So far, there had been no sign of Emil, and she could tell that Laurent was still overcoming his jealousy of Jean Claude.

He'd wanted the truth, so she'd given it to him. She wasn't going to sugar coat things for him. Better he knew the truth, or as much of it as she remembered.

Laurent trapped her hands beneath his. She smiled against his shoulder.

"I think I'm starting to get the hang of making biscuits," she murmured, hoping to make him feel better.

He laughed. "I'm glad you're feeling more at home."

"Me too." She was glad she'd come to a truce with Jules. And that André and Burke accepted her. That she'd found friends in Amanda and Angelica. Real friends. Friends she could laugh with. It felt so good to laugh.

She felt him reading her mind and knew that he wasn't feeling as jubilant as she was.

He was silent for several moments and then he sighed.

"Are you ever going to tell me the name of the man who hired you to kill me?

She'd kept that truth from him long enough. And she was tired of the secrets that had held her hostage for so long. "It wasn't a man."

"It was a woman?" Laurent frowned. Who had he pissed off? He'd had his share of affairs, but he'd always made sure they were happy even after he left. "Her name?"

"Marie Bernard-Deveraux."

"My aunt Marie? Are you joking?" He spun around.

She shrugged. "How would I know?"

Damn. She was right. She wouldn't know the names of his family back in France. But this news…

He pulled on a pair of worn jeans, then grabbed a shirt off of the chair. Turning on his heel, he stormed out of the room. The old wooden floor boards creaked under his weight as he stalked downstairs.

"Sebastian," he said, entering the kitchen. "I have the name." He buttoned the shirt.

Sebastian put down his mug and stood, his dark eyes going stormy. "Who is it?"

"Your mother."

"What?" his cousin asked, incredulous. By his reaction, Laurent was sure that even with the bad blood between him and his mother, Sebastian was going to come out swinging.

"Cayenne said the woman who hired her to kill me was Marie Bernard-Deveraux. Do you know anyone else by that name?"

Sebastian's fists turned white, but he kept them by his sides. There were too many questions left unanswered. Too many coincidences lately.

"Why does she want me dead?" Laurent asked. "I thought she hated *you.*"

"I have no idea. Are you sure you heard—"

"Correctly? Yes."

"Perhaps she's lyin'."

Laurent's temper flared and he cut his eyes at his cousin. "Why would she do that?"

"To cause problems? I don't know."

He'd thought they'd left that world behind. Life in Europe with their pack had been a supernatural soap opera.

They'd started over. Started fresh…without the violence. Without the vengeance. But it seemed to have followed them.

"I haven't spoken to my moth—Marie Bernard-Deveraux in years," Sebastian said quietly. He had that far away look in his eyes and Laurent assumed that his cousin didn't even remember the last time he'd spoken to his mother. He'd probably lost count of the years, as Laurent had.

From the corner of his eye he saw a dark figure at the edge of the yard. "Where's Burke?" he asked, but he already knew the answer.

"In the den, I guess." Sebastian frowned. "Why?"

"They're here."

Sebastian cursed as he stepped across the kitchen and flipped off the lights. Centuries old instincts kicked in, putting Laurent on high alert. In his heart he'd known Emil wouldn't let Cayenne go without a fight. Laurent couldn't really blame the vamp. Laurent would fight to the death for her.

Lightning lit the room and Laurent saw a look in Sebastian's eyes that he'd never seen before. Always the consummate Alpha of their pack, Sebastian was a strong leader. A fierce warrior. Fearless.

Marrying Amanda had changed him. In more ways than the obvious. He'd never, in all the years Laurent had known him, had fear in his eyes.

But then, the love of a woman changed a man. Soothed the beast. Laurent felt that familiar ache in his chest. Not from love. But from the fear of losing Violet—Cayenne again. Once in a lifetime was more than enough.

Cayenne? He reached out with his mind.

I see them, she replied.

He stepped to the side of the window to watch their opponent approach. "I count two," he whispered. Thunder rattled the window panes.

"Two more out front," Sebastian said quietly

from the other side of the room. "They've got us surrounded."

Laurent nodded. "Go protect Amanda," he urged.

The tension in the air was thicker than the humidity in a summer swamp. Sebastian wasted no time and headed off into the darkness.

Laurent continued to watch the windows, letting the beast inside him hover just below the surface. A few well place swipes with his claws and those vamps would be dead.

He heard a thump from somewhere in the center of the house and moved toward it.

One down, Sebastian's deep voice filled his mind.

André chimed in. *Two dead on this side of da house.*

Laurent held his breath as he heard the floorboards creak in the hallway. He saw a gun and the pencil thin vampire holding it. Lightning lit the room but the illumination came to late.

Laurent's claws sliced through the vampires neck and his body hit the ground.

They must have sent in the dumb ones, Laurent informed the others.

A loud crash on the second floor had Laurent racing toward the stairs.

When Laurent pushed open his door, he found Cayenne spinning through the air, her sword drawn. A vamp stood at the foot of the bed trying to catch her in the sights of his gun. Before Laurent could move, change, or even growl, she'd taken down her opponent. His head fell to the floor with a thud. The vamp's body crumbled into a heap and then turned to powder.

"Let's go," he told her and started for the hallway.

A bullet splintered the door frame.

"This way," she called.

He slammed the door and shoved the dresser in front of it for good measure. The window shattered like a bomb hit it. He turned just in time to see his favorite chair sail through the air. She gave him an apologetic shrug and stepped onto the ledge.

Adrenaline surged through his bloodstream as he surveyed the ground. A ball of flame hurtled through the air below. A window in Sebastian's room shattered and fumes assaulted his nose.

Fire!

Everyone out, Cayenne added.

More bullets drove them out the window onto the roof of the porch below.

Laurent pulled her to him and gave her a fierce kiss before he leapt off the roof. He landed in a crouch; she, in a lunge. He spotted Sebastian sprinting towards the grove of trees behind the house, with Amanda thrown over his shoulder.

The vampire who'd thrown the torch into the house rushed him. Laurent let his beast rush forward another notch and caught the vamp around the middle. He flipped the vamp over his head and turned to finish him off. But Cayenne was already there, her sword slicing through the air. The vampire's head hit the dirt just before his body.

"Come on." They needed to develop a new plan with the others.

Laurent put one foot in front of the other and raced toward the tree line. Cayenne matched him stride for stride. He hissed out a breath as a bullet tore through his arm, but he didn't slow down. A huge wolf raced by them at a dead run. *Burke.*

They met Sebastian, Jules, and Burke in the thick of the woods. When he turned back toward the house, all he saw was a flaming structure and smoke filling the sky. Rage surged through him, and the beast inside him demanded release.

A raindrop smacked his cheek, and he smelled the storm closing in.

"Those bastards," Amanda yelled.

"You're hit," Cayenne said, her gaze fixed on the blood oozing through Laurent's shirt sleeve.

"I'll live."

A crash drew their attention back to the house. A body landed on the lawn, and a were-wolf leapt on top of it.

"André," Sebastian whispered.

Laurent watched his cousin, now part man, part wolf, close his massive jaws around the vamp's head and give it a good shake. Even from this distance, he could see blood and hear the bones crush.

Beside him, Cayenne sucked in a breath. He pulled her to his side and let his gaze sweep over the yard.

"You need to go. Take Amanda and Angel with you," Laurent told her. Two more vamps rounded the corner just as André disappeared behind the garage.

She shook her head quickly. "You guys, go. I need to finish this." Cayenne pulled her hair back into a ponytail.

"Like hell you will," Laurent said.

"Just go. You're wounded."

"Not anymore." He ripped the sleeve off his shirt to show he was already healed.

"We're not letting you fight alone," Jules said. His cousin's words surprised him. But someone needed to make sure Amanda and Angel were safe.

"Go with Burke," Sebastian told Amanda and Angelica. "He's the fastest." The two human women didn't look like they were going to budge. In fact, Amanda looked angry enough to rip off someone's head. But when André came through the trees, towering, half furry, with a wolf's snout and claws at the ends of his fingers, and a sword in his hand they raced further into the woods with Burke on their heels.

Laurent let his beast take over and endured the painful tearing of muscle, the popping and contracting of his bones. His vision got better, as did his hearing and sense of smell. His clothes disintegrated around him, and he dared not look at the woman next to him.

He let out a low growl, and it was matched by the three werewolves to his left. A feminine growl lifted to his ears, and he jerked his gaze to the right. Cayenne's eyes were silver; her fangs, long and glistening white. The corners of her ruby lips were pulled into a grin.

She looked deadly. And hauntingly beautiful.

"So I don't sound quite as intimidating," she said simply, then flicked her gaze back to the field where the vamps were lining up.

Your mate has spunk, I'll give her that. Jules words whispered through his mind.

But can she fight? Sebastian asked.

"Watch and see boys," Cayenne said aloud. "Watch and see."

And then she was gone.

While they started through the woods slowly, sticking close to the trees, sizing up their opponents, Cayenne moved with supernatural speed, meeting her adversary like a streak of lightning sent down from the sky.

The vamps advanced on them with their guns drawn. Two of them headed for Laurent.

Lightning splintered the night sky and lit up

the yard like a football stadium. When the vamps were finally within the grove, he turned to his cousins. A silent message passed between them, and they spread out. *André and I will take the front*, Sebastian said.

A bullet whizzed by Laurent's head. The bastard never even saw Sebastian coming. More shots rang out and the battle began. Over the gunfire, Laurent heard a vamp cry out and turned to see Cayenne wielding her sword with deadly accuracy. Another vamp approached, his bony finger on the trigger of his weapon, but her speed and grace let her sidestep the bullets.

A roar echoed through the trees, and Laurent focused his attention on the enemy. An enemy who didn't see him coming until it was too late. His claws sliced through the vamp's skin, severing his head. Another bullet hit him in the shoulder.

He spun, his claws extended, and found another vamp advancing on him. He dove through the air, his muscles coiled, ready for another blow. A quick swipe, and his opponent's gun dropped to the ground. Laurent bowled him over. They rolled, a heavy mass of swinging arms and kicking legs. Laurent's claws sliced the vamp's flesh, and he cried out. The creature clenched his strong hand around Laurent's throat, and he glared down into the vamp's eerie silver eyes.

He snarled, baring his teeth.

"No!" The vampire's scream filled his ears as

Laurent pressed down to finish off the creature. His blood was bitter.

The clang of swords drew his attention. His heart almost stopped when he saw Cayenne crumpled to the ground.

At that moment, the sky opened up. A crescendo of rain and thunder filled the air as Laurent ran toward his mate.

Cayenne's torso ached from the blow Emil had dealt her. She tightened her grip on the sword and waited from his approach. That was always Emil's downfall. Advancing, when he should retreat. She tightened her muscles, ready to spring to life.

One more step. He raised his sword. She watched him through her lashes.

"It didn't have to come to this Cayenne," he shouted over the storm. "Or should I call you Violet?" His eyes were swirling orbs of silver.

A back flip threw her out of harm's way, but she made sure the tip of her boot connected with his chin. His head snapped back with a satisfying crack.

"Now we're even," she told him as she landed lightly on her feet.

From the corner of her eye, she saw Laurent running full tilt toward Emil. His jaws were locked, and a determined glint lit his eyes. Emil must have heard him, because he spun, his sword flying. A mass of claws, teeth, and fur, Laurent landed on him with an inhuman roar. Cayenne watched, her heart in her throat. There was so much blood. So many grunts and groans as they rolled and fought.

A sharp pain tore through her chest as Laurent backed up and she saw the damage he'd done to Emil. A combination of happiness, sadness, anxiety, and ire filled her. The bonds were gone. Freedom. Memories. Her past life. Her youth. It was all there in her mind rushing in like water filling a canyon.

But Emil…He was supposed to be *her* kill. It was for her to finish.

Laurent dropped to his knees and turned his pained eyes to her as he slipped back into his human form. Emil's dagger stuck out from his chest. A startled cry tore from her lips, and she dove to catch him as he collapsed. She cradled him in her arms and stared into the brown eyes she'd grown to love.

"You crazy, crazy man," she cried, her words muffled against his cheek.

"Cayenne—"

"For goodness sake, call me Violet." A puzzled look crossed his face. "I never much liked the name Cayenne anyway; it's what Emil always called me."

"Violet." Her name came out on a sigh, and he cupped her cheek with one big, bloodied palm. Her heart beat violently in her chest.

"That was supposed to be *my* kill. My hundredth. You'd better get your health back so I can whollop you."

"*Whollop* me?"

She grinned, realizing Amanda's favorite expression had made it into her vocabulary.

"Damn, I love you," he said, sounding pained.

"Should I pull it out?" she asked, frowning at the dagger. Werewolf physiology wasn't her forte. He dropped his head back, his eyes dazed. "Don't you dare die on me, Laurent. Don't you dare. André!"

Her shout echoed through the woods. She hardly noticed the water showering down over them until she saw it washing away the blood. Vital blood.

"I love you, you big beast. Don't you die," she repeated, hugging him tighter. She was closer to tears than she could ever remember being.

André dropped to her side and inspected the man in her arms.

"Lay him flat."

As gently as she could, she followed his orders. He pulled the blade free and flung it deep into the woods.

"We've got to stop the bleeding. It will speed his healing."

Healing. Such a beautiful word. So fitting. For her, and for Laurent.

André pressed his hands against the wound.

She tugged her shirt over her head and offered it to him. The rain pelted her skin, stinging her.

"How is he?" Jules asked, coming through the grove. Sebastian halted beside him.

"He's unconscious. But he'll be fine."

"I'll go get Burke and the girls." Jules headed into the trees.

Sebastian collapsed next to Laurent.

She met his gaze. "I'm sorry I brought this upon you."

"We've had worse."

She turned and looked at the smoldering house.

"The sprinklers put most of it out. It can be rebuilt, Violet."

Suddenly numb, she nodded.

Without warning, the man between them came alive, striking out and sending Sebastian and André flying. Violet rolled backwards and landed in a crouch. Laurent growled low in his throat, and she saw the change happening to him as he went from human to werewolf in the blink of an eye.

He faced her in a lunge, his brown eyes bright in the darkness. When his gaze focused on her, his features softened. His posture relaxed, and he stopped growling.

"I should have mentioned he'd be a little grouchy when he first wakes up," André called over the thunder.

Laurent dropped to his knees, his bare chest perfect and whole once again. The fur disappeared, and his bones compacted until he was human. One very handsome human. The rain had washed the blood away.

She launched herself into his arms.

"Let's go find the rest of the pack, André," Sebastian said, his voice distant.

"Do I remember hearing something about *love* coming from those beautiful lips of yours?" Laurent asked softly, kissing her cheeks, her neck, and everywhere in between.

"You did. I thought you were unconscious."

"Almost." He fused their lips together in a kiss that stole her breath and spoke of years of missed kisses. Rain helped their hands glide over each other's skin as they touched and caressed.

She trailed a hand over the place where the mating mark rested. His heart beat solidly beneath her palm. Assured that he really was fine, she wrapped her arms around his broad shoulders.

A familiar flutter started in her stomach and radiated outward.

"We're going to get a hotel room," Jules called out.

"I'll clean up this mess and deal with the fire department. You guys should get out of here," Burke said and strolled off toward the garage.

"We'll catch you later," Laurent said, lifting

his head a fraction. She smiled and pulled him back to her. "He's right. There's a hurricane coming—"

"I'm sick of hurricanes. Last week. This week. Let's go somewhere where there aren't any hurricanes," she whispered against his lips. Needing to be closer, they sank to the ground.

"We really have to stop doing this in the rain."

"I don't think we should stop at all," he murmured against her throat. A delicious shiver raced over her skin, and she eagerly arched against his hand when she slipped it beneath the button of her jeans.

"Mmm...you're right." She closed her eyes and concentrated on the sensations flowing through her and the happy memories they were creating to add to past great memories. Like pictures in a photo album, she saw her past. Memories flashed by as if they'd never been missing. Her childhood. Laurent. His family. Her family.

The night she died.

She shook her head, not wanting to remember that part.

"My memories..."

"Are they back?"

She didn't open her eyes; she only nodded.

"I thought Emil might have cast a spell on you. What do you remember?"

"Only how badly I need you inside me." She smiled.

His groan was drowned out by a loud clap of thunder. She reached between them and cupped his cock. He was hard and ready, just the way she liked him.

Her pussy grew moist at the thought of him settling between her legs, of them making love. She gave him a squeeze and was rewarded with more groans of pleasure.

He trailed kisses over her skin as he worked off her jeans. The soaked fabric made it difficult, but she lifted her hips to help. A stick poked her in the shoulder, and she tried to ignore it.

Then Laurent knelt between her legs and glided his palms back and forth over her thighs. "Mine."

"I was just thinking the same about you."

His gentle fingers stroked the tender folds between her legs. She tipped her pelvis to give him better access. He slid one thick finger inside her pussy and grazed her clit with his thumb. She dug her fingers into the damp earth, silently willing him to bring her to the peak of pleasure. The slow in and out motion of his finger and the lazy circles of his thumb reminded her of torture. A very slow, exacting torture with one purpose—to drive her mad with want.

Mind and body, she was anxious. Ready. Every nerve ending screamed for completion...and more contact. She felt her way to his cock and gave it a hard squeeze. In the cold rain, it was hot like lava. She craved the feel of his big, warm body almost as much as she craved the orgasm that built slowly between her legs.

"Warm me up, big boy." She gave his member a gentle tug to drive her point home.

He withdrew his fingers immediately and settled himself over her. She opened her eyes and blinked back the rain drops. His hair was a wet, sexy mess, and he slid his body easily over hers.

She hiked a leg over his hip, opening her body to his. Once his arms were bracketed around her, his chest brushing her breasts and his cock poised at her entrance, a sense of rightness washed over her. A sense of home. In a field, drenched by rain, or in a bed...it didn't matter. Just so long as she was with him. Beneath him. Wrapped around him.

He kissed her chin, then her jaw. She turned, met his lips with hers, and grabbed his butt. Flexing her fingers into his taunt flesh, she speared her tongue between his lips and pulled him inside her. His weight pressed her into the dirt, but she didn't mind. In fact, she welcomed it, her body eagerly cradling his as he slowly withdrew and then pressed into her again. She broke the kiss and watched the emotions play across his face as he surged in and out of her.

Perfection. The way she'd always dreamed it

would be. Two hundred years and several thousand miles ago, she'd been a young woman in love...and in desire. She'd waited for him, for something that had never come to fruition.

Until now.

She broke the kiss. "We've waited a long time for this," she said softly.

"Uh-huh." Concentration hardened his features. In and out he moved, faster and faster, delighting her eager nerve endings and building a climax within her.

Delicious. The word rang through her mind over and over.

Delicious. Delicious. Delicious.

The differences between them had never been more apparent. Or more beautiful. The way her body tightened around him and softened beneath him. The energy and stamina his wolf provided. The endurance and insatiable desire she'd been given as a vampire.

They were perfectly matched. She would never deny it again.

"I won't let you."

"Reading my mind again, wolf?" She arched against him, and he ducked his head to nibble the tender skin of her neck.

"Always, *mon amour*," he whispered. "Always."

"I'm sorry."

"For what?"

"Disappearing on you. Wasting two hundred years."

"It doesn't matter. You're here now…and that's what...matters." His breathlessness made her smile. She wrapped her legs around his waist and held on for the ride. His movements were so hard, so fast, that she actually moved across the wet ground.

With a sound she'd come to expect and thought uniquely his own, he groaned. His muscles coiled and his cock swelled deep inside as he emptied himself into her. The pressure against her clit was enough to set her off as well, and she gave a cry of her own. Her pussy clenched and released around his cock as her whole body melted in ecstasy.

"Hmm..."

"I agree." He rolled to the side and pulled her on top of him.

"I'm still going to whollop you," she told him, pressing herself against him from shoulder to knee.

"You promise?"

"Absolutely," she whispered against his lips. And then she kissed him. It was a kiss that poured out her heart and spoke of all the living they still had to do together in this life, all the love she'd finally found.

And when he returned her kiss, she knew that he, too, had finally found his reason for living.

No one loves more deeply that André Deveraux. And no one feels the sting of rejection more than the stoic werewolf everyone relies on. It's finally his turn at happily ever after…with the most unlikely match.

Enjoy this excerpt from Mated to a Cajun Werewolf.

"It looks like this is going to be a doozy of a storm, folks. Hurricane Love is skirting Florida's east coast right now, roaring north at fifteen miles per hour. The storm will likely make landfall between Jacksonville, Florida and Charleston, South Carolina. Cities along the coast are now under a full voluntary evacuation. Paul, how are things looking in the Weather Center?"

André Deveraux glanced up from the book in his lap and studied the gray haired man on the television screen. Behind him a large map of the Southeast showed the first of bands of rain moving across Savannah. The wide mass of swirling clouds looked imposing, even to André.

He'd gotten to the airport hours in advance of his flight with hopes of catching an earlier one, but the airport was clogged with travelers and the plane/passenger ratio was not good. The Bobs, Deveraux Shipping's lawyers, had been smart to catch a flight late last night. André had wanted another night to himself, to think over his future. Not that the extra time had helped.

"Hurricane Love is picking up speed, Don. And the barometer continues to drop. South Florida is already experiencing heavy rain from this storm. Fort Lauderdale has picked up two and a half inches in the last six hours. If you're in the path of this storm, I strongly urge you to get out of the way." The man made a sweeping motion with his hand, away from the coast.

Easier said than done, buddy.

A sharp ring and the accompanying vibration alerted him to a call. He dug his cell phone out of his pants pocket and glanced at the number. *Angel-*

ica. A sharp ache squeezed his heart and headed south.

He pressed the answer button and held it to his ear. "Hi, Angel."

"Hiya, handsome. We were wondering if you were able to catch an earlier flight."

He glanced at his luggage, still sitting in the same spot at his feet where he'd dropped it three hours ago.

"No. There weren't any earlier flights."

A long pause clued him in to Angelica's worry. Ever since that week in the cabin when he and Jules had brought her in out of the storm he'd had a connection with her. Past what was normal for a brother and sister-in-law. But she'd made her choice. It was Jules who'd stolen her heart. And André had stepped out of the picture.

"I'll be fine, Angel. Don't worry about me."

"I can't help but worry about you. You won't let anyone take care of you."

"That's because I don't need taking care of," he clipped. That wasn't entirely true, and he knew it. He saw what Angelica had with Jules and Sebastian with Amanda and it made him crave that closeness for himself. He was no longer used to the yearning that plagued him. He didn't like it. Didn't like wanting anything as much as he wanted a woman of his own. Someone to hold close, someone who would dote on him, be excited to see him, someone to share his life, his wealth with. But that woman was not Angel. "I didn't mean to be short with you."

"I know," she said quietly. She probably did. Angelica Humphrey was an amazing woman, easy-going, expressive, giving. Perfect in so many ways. And she fit seamlessly into Pack life.

"Any progress on the house?" he asked, hoping that questions about something other than him would ease some of the growing tension. When their home had burnt to the ground last month, Sebastian, his older brother and the Alpha of their pack, had declared that they would rebuild. Construction had already begun.

"Sebastian's looking for a supplier of old flooring. There was a reporter snooping around the other day but Gin and Burke ran him off. They've almost got the roof on."

She continued talking, telling him about the plans that Amanda and Sebastian, the pack's Alphas, were making. Only half listening, he heard something about overstuffed furniture, rocking chairs and a nursery.

He watched the TV screen and the storm that was heading to shore. Just then a voice came over the loudspeaker announcing that all flights had been canceled due to weather.

"Angel..." he interrupted. She fell silent. "They just canceled my flight. I have to go. Talk to you soon."

"Okay. Love ya. Be careful."

"You too."

He ended the call and stared at the phone for several seconds. That ache was still there nestled in his heart. He'd dwelled on their relationship far longer than he should have. The pact with Jules didn't extend to mates. And even if it did, he just didn't love Angel with an all-consuming passion. He'd only felt that with one woman. The one woman he could never have.

Gathering his luggage, he headed back to the rental car counter where he'd dropped off the keys to the SUV a few hours ago. Somehow, he had to get out of here. His business was rapped up. The sale was going to go through. Sebastian would be pleased. Negotiating the throng of people, he wondered what they would do once they were no longer the owners of Deveraux Shipping.

For the last decade they'd thrown themselves into their business and for a time it had made their bachelorhood tolerable. But lately there had been a gnawing at André's gut reminding him that there was more to life than making money.

Maybe he'd travel. He'd never been to Canada or Antarctica. Maybe a world cruise was in order. He'd definitely have to consider that once he got back to Louisiana.

As he stepped up to the car rental counter, he caught a whiff of perfume mixed with warm, alluring woman. But it was distinctively werewolf too. The delicious scent teased his memory, tormenting him.

Man, he had it worse than he thought. White hot lust coursed through his veins and his cock twitched to life. Just being in the same part of the country and he was thinking he could smell her—

"What do you mean you have no other cars? As in none?" A feminine voice floated down the expanse to him. There was a trace of accent, French, and a barely controlled panic.

His head swiveled left toward the sound, and he caught sight of the woman in all her furious glory. A mane of long mahogany waves cascaded over her shoulders. The silky strands made his fingers itch to sweep them from her face. His gaze swooped lower, taking in the sophisticated charcoal gray dress that hugged her tall curvy frame like denim fresh from the dryer. Her legs, pale and bare of pantyhose, went on for miles. She wore ultra-sexy, black leather heels. And her toes, dear God, the perfectly painted red polish did crazy things to his mind.

At the same moment, his body tensed and his heart dropped. He knew the woman without having to look at her face. She'd have wide blue eyes, a perfect nose—minus the old break—and ruby red lips. She was pretty without being overly beautiful. Her special blend of quiet assurance and subtle seduction could have a man eating out of the palm of her hand with a single lick of her lips.

André knew that, knew *her*, all too well. Juliette Vassar was the one woman in all of Savannah, *non*...the world, that he'd hoped to avoid on this trip. He'd sworn to himself that he would not search her out and yet here she was. Were the stars in alignment? Were the Fates playing tricks on him?

She flicked her hair over her shoulder, showing off the creamy column of her neck. He swallowed a groan and slowly traced the profile he knew so well.

"Fuck me," he muttered.

"Was that an invitation?" André jerked his gaze to the short blonde behind the counter. She gave him a willing smile.

He raised an eyebrow and then sat his briefcase at his feet. "I'm going to need the SUV again." He tried not to notice the disappointment in her eyes.

How the hell was he going to get out of here without Juliette seeing him? Like him, she had a killer sense of smell, and he was willing to bet his life that she still felt the bond between them just like he did.

It would pull them together like magnets if he let it. All those years ago, they hadn't just been in love. He hadn't just worshiped the ground she walked on, adored and desired her. *Non.* He'd mated with her. For life.

Overhead a voice blared through a speaker. "The weather service has issued a voluntary hurricane evacuation—"

"Great," André muttered as the crowd around him surged into chaos.

"If you'll sign here, Mr. Deveraux." He took the pen she offered and scrawled his signature on the line.

"What about you? Do you have any cars left?" Juliette's voice was closer this time. André grabbed the keys to his rental and turned to gather his things. His gut tightened into little knots. *Just turn around and walk away.*

But he couldn't. Sighing, he turned back to see her blue eyes glimmering with hope and a hint of desperation.

"No, ma'am. I'm afraid not," the attendant said in a thick southern accent. André didn't like the way the man behind the counter ogled Juliette. Didn't like it one little bit. But he pushed the feeling aside and picked up his briefcase.

One by one the counters closed.

"I can take you wherever you need to go, *cheri.*"

Finish Andre's story. Buy Mated to a Cajun Werewolf today!

If you enjoyed Laurent & Violet's story, please let your fellow readers know by rating and/or reviewing at your favorite bookseller's website or your favorite book community. Reviews help more than you know.

JOIN SELENA'S WOLFPACK

Become a part of Selena's community of book lovers, the Wolfpack. You'll receive her newsletter, SELENA SAYS, right in your inbox and stay up to date on all her:

- latest releases
- sales
- freebies

Speaking of freebies, sign up right now and get access to her Free Read Library! http://www.selena-blake.com/newsletter/

OTHER BOOKS BY SELENA BLAKE

Series: Paranormal Protectors: New Orleans

Bewitched by His Fated Mate

Claiming His Forbidden Witch

Resisting the Vampire's Kiss

Capturing His Wicked Witch

Series: Stormy Weather

The Cajun Werewolf's Captive

Bitten in the Bayou

Seduced by a Cajun Werewolf

Mated to a Cajun Werewolf

Stranded with a Cajun Werewolf

A Cajun Werewolf Christmas

Series: Mystic Isle

Fangs, Fur & Forever

A Werewolf to Call Her Own

Games Demons Play

Pursued by a Werewolf

Bound to the Vampire

Anthologies

Stormy Weather Collector's Edition (5-in-1, plus interviews, deleted scenes and more)

Mystic Isle

Short Stories

Kissing Wilde

Single Titles

Ready & Willing - There can be only one alpha.

♥ ♥ ♥

Selena writes contemporary romance and romantic suspense under the name Gillian Blakely.

ABOUT THE AUTHOR

An action movie buff with a penchant for all things supernatural and sexy, Selena Blake combines her love for adventure, travel and romance into steamy paranormal romance. Selena's books have been called "a steamy escape" and have appeared on bestseller lists, been nominated for awards, and won contests. When she's not writing you can find her by the pool soaking up some sun, day dreaming about new characters, and watching the cabana boy (aka her muse), Derek. Fan mail keeps her going when the diet soda wears off so write to her at Selena@selena-blake.com

Newsletter
http://www.selena-blake.com/newsletter

Stay In Touch
selena-blake.com
selena@selena-blake.com

Printed in Great Britain
by Amazon